W9-CHI-609

Haunts &Taunts

Haunts & Taunts

A book for Hallowe'en and
all the nights of the year

Jean Chapman

Illustrated by **VAL BIRO**

Song Settings by
Margaret Moore

AWARD PUBLICATIONS LIMITED

ISBN 0-86163-700-3

Text copyright © 1976 Jean Chapman
Illustrations copyright © 1993 Award Publications Limited
Musical setting © 1976 Hodder and Stoughton Australia Pty Ltd

This edition first published 1994

Published by Award Publications Limited,
1st Floor, Goodyear House,
52-56 Osnaburgh Street, London NW1 3NS

Printed in Spain

INTRODUCTION

Boggles and ghaisties,
And four-legged beasties,
And things that go *bump*
In the night.

The Scary Ones and their more benevolent kin belong to our imaginations, an inheritance passed on from pre-history and the darker times when people, once night fell, had no light other than a flickering fire, wavering candles or dim rush-lights which threw deceitful shadows. Outside the cave or hut, in the great spreading darkness, nameless Things shifted and scratched, pattered or squealed, snarled, hooted and howled. Fear of the unknown and of natural phenomena created a horde of fantastic creatures with superhuman powers. Many still exist in old customs, traditional stories, rhymes and songs although the original superstitions and symbols are forgotten, or vaguely remembered. "A fairy tale never dies" wrote Hans Christian Andersen. Strong plots and pertinent values have assisted the survival of the best stories, many of which were first told to adults, then purloined by the children, irrespective of adult opinion. And our children read or listen, shedding the cloak of disbelief in a complete involvement which often extends their knowledge of human behaviour and values, and on occasions helps a troubled child to come to terms with a personal bogy.

Nevertheless, for the youngest children who can't yet differentiate between reality and make-believe, stories should be selected with care. Although an age-guide is arbitrary, our anthology is best suited for children of seven and over. This is the great fairy-tale age and the fortunate never quite leave it behind, and so the request for a collection of "spooky spine-tinglers" came from seven-year-olds and "friends".

"It's only a fairy tale" is a catch phrase we all hear, and admittedly, characterization is seldom convincing. Values are. And so, we have Katie Crackernuts and her devotion to her cruelly mis-used step-sister and the ailing Prince, Gilly's sacrificing love for Nicht Nought Nothing, the young wife whose ignorance brings Brownie grief and the right of Granny to live her own life even if others are intolerant. All are meaningful to children who absorb and interpret.

But what of the idealistic endings to the tales, the false promises of living "happily ever after"? It's just not true, critics argue. Well now, apart from the fact that children — and some adults, like a neat and satisfying ending, the trials and tests besetting the characters must be endured or conquered before rewards are *earned*. "Happily ever after" symbolises emotional and physical maturity, the capability of facing the future with personal strengths.

Another criticism which can be justified is the horrific content of some stories; a reminder that the stories were once adult fare. Yet small children suffer griefs which are often more intense and disturbing than the emotions of adults experienced by longer years of living. Fairy-tale violence, unless tampered with, almost always is intrinsic to the plot's development. It is stated, then the story proceeds. It is never over-proportioned, and sadly, violence is a truth of life.

Jean Chapman

For
Louise and Roslyn and Gregory,
and Robyn and Ruff and Phee,
Erica, Roberta and Peter,
and for you.

CONTENTS

Key to Symbols for contents
⅄ = story   ☆ = verse
🖐 = activity   ☻ = song

NIGHT NOISES

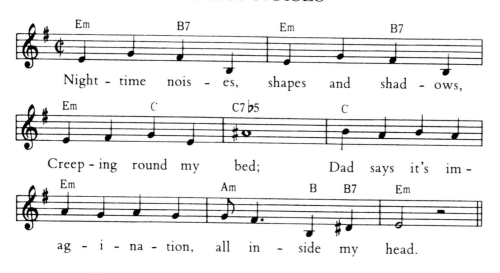

Night - time nois - es, shapes and shad - ows,

Creep - ing round my bed; Dad says it's im -

ag - i - na - tion, all in - side my head.

I hear something big and furry
Creeping round the house;
I'm so frightened, please what is it?
. . . Silly, it's a mouse.

Two green eyes are at the window
Staring at the mat;
I'm so frightened, please what is it?
. . . Silly, it's a cat.

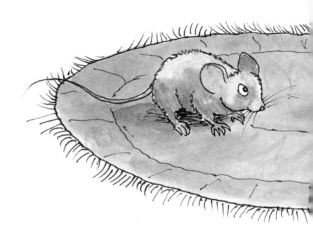

I can see enormous fingers
Pointing right at me;
I'm so frightened, please what is it?
 . . . Silly, it's a tree.

I can see a great white face that's
Looking in my room;
I'm so frightened, please what is it?
 . . . Silly, it's the moon.

Night-time noises, shapes and shadows,
Couldn't hurt a flea;
They were just imagination,
All made up by me.
                    Joy Moore and Raymond Long

13

CHANT OF THE BEANSTALK GIANT

Fee-fi-fo-fum!
I smell the blood of an Englishman!
Be he live, or be he dead,
I'll grind his bones to make my bread.

Often giants, so enormous in size and strength and wickedness, were stupid. Not all! A few were kindly and foolish. Even so, except in your imagination, you will not meet Cuchullin or Finn, or even Sneezy Snatcher, or do you know him already? Sometimes he's called Mr Miacca.

14

THE GIANT WHO SUCKED HIS THUMB

Once, in the time of long ago, the strongest Giant in all of Ireland was Cuchullin. He could snatch a thunderbolt from the sky, squash it flat like a pancake, then spin it like a plate over the Atlantic Ocean. And that trick alone was enough to scare the neighbourhood giants into a state of jelly-knees and custard-elbows. Not only did they stay out of Cuchullin's sight, they kept way out of ear-shot too. Well away! Otherwise that bumptious loud-mouthed blustering bully-boy of a hooligan would be calling before breakfast, yelling for a fight. Cuchullin was a belt-cuff-swing-slam fighter, he was. He pummelled, punched, clouted and kicked his victim over the mountains and into England. By the time the poor bruised wretch limped home it was long past breakfast, and his bannocks were cold.

However, there was just *one* giant fellow who had not been frightened by Cuchullin's shenanigans. That was Finn, himself. To be sure, Finn was smart enough to keep out of Cuchullin's way. Half a country away! A-top his own high mountain from where he had a fine view of both the

15

countryside and Cuchullin's doings! When that conceited young ruffian appeared like a speck on the horizon Finn was off on urgent business, such as salmon fishing, or trout tickling or chasing wild boars in the bog.

Cuchullin was forever seeking Finn. He determined not to rest until he had fought him and so mastered every giant in the land. But that pesky fox-sly Finn kept hiding away and spoiling his record.

Now, little did Cuchullin know that Finn possessed a precious gift. His thumb it was. A magical thumb! Finn had only to put it into his mouth, give it a suck and his marvellous thumb flashed messages which were as clear as day to Finn and to Finn only.

So, by chance one morning, Finn popped his thumb into his mouth to clean some grit from his teeth when he had a flash vision which sent him scurrying pell-mell to his wife. "Oonah! Oonah!" he bleated. "Cuchullin's on the march and after me bones. Me thumb tells me there'll be no escapin' this time."

"Stop shaking like a leaf in the wind, me lovely boy!" she said. Oh, Oonah was a sensible darling if ever there was one. "What time can we be expecting the savage young blusterer?" she wanted to know.

Finn pushed his thumb into his mouth and sucked. *Spppt!* "Me thumb says, two o'clock today. And Oonah, Windbags Cuchullin is boastin' that he'll break and flatten me, then kick me into France."

"Love of me heart, Finn Darlin', will you leave this to me?" crooned Oonah. "There's a way that I be knowing which will put you out of the clutches of this wild villain before you ever get into them. So will you be doin' what I ask now, Finn?"

16

"Yes," Finn promised and she hustled him out of the house whilst she prepared for their visitor.

Down the mountain she clattered to borrow a griddle-iron from every neighbour, every one of them people-sized, just as we are nowadays. Not one feared Oonah and she was wider than a barn and taller than the church steeple. Imagine it! But Oonah's heart was soft and sweet like a creamy-centred chocolate, and as big as her generous self. So, up the mountain she clanked with twenty-one heavy griddle-irons in her apron.

She whipped and she beat and made *twenty-four* cakes, thick with currants and sugared on top. Plumb in the middle of twenty-one cakes she baked a griddle-iron, and they looked exactly the same as the three without a centre of hard, black iron. And the lovely appetising eat-again smell of them drifted down the mountainside with the breeze so that far-off Cuchullin himself whiffed them.

At round about two o'clock she saw him coming — away, away in the distance, like a black dot in the middle of a cloud of dust bowling over the fields. The closer the dust cloud rolled the bigger grew both it and Cuchullin.

"Come now, Finn! Make haste! Cuchullin is comin'. It's time you dressed for our guest," she called, dragging a cradle from under the bed. It was bigger than a shed it was, but she deftly parked it by the stove, then helped Finn to dress.

Over his head she hauled one of her daisy-white, lace-flounced nightgowns. On his head she pulled one of her floppy-frilled, ribbon-tied, sheeny silk, pale blue nightcaps. She helped Finn into the cradle and while he scrunched down she covered him with an embroidered quilt as big as a barley field. "There you are, my own precious babby!" clucked Oonah tickling him under his chin. "Not a word from you I want now. Just suck your thumb, and you'll know what's going to happen and what I'll be needing you to do. But first, me darlin', let your thumb tell where Cuchullin keeps his great strength."

Slppppt! Finn sucked long and hard. "In the finger, the very middle finger of his right hand!" scowled Finn. "Let me at him! Without that finger he'd have no strength at all, he wouldn't."

"Tush-hush! Wait now!" Oonah hissed a warning. "It's himself comin' to the door."

Hearing Cuchullin's wallops on Finn's door, the folk in the valley feared an earthquake. The very land under their feet shook until with a smile, Oonah opened her door. "Come in and welcome," she greeted Cuchullin. "What can I be doin' for you then?"

"Is this where the mighty Finn himself lives?" boomed Cuchullin.

"It is that. I'm his wife, and here in the cradle is little Finn."

"And a bonny babby is your little Finn," said Cuchullin with a glance at the cradle. "Where is his Dadda now?"

"Somewhere or the other. He's keeping his eyes open for that blather-mouth Cuchullin. Finn's heard that Cuchullin is boastin' that he'll throw him over the sea to France." Oonah chuckled. "If my Finn catches bully-tough Cuchullin first, he'll turn him into dogmeat."

"Will he now!" rumbled Cuchullin. "I'm thinkin' it'll be the other way round. I'm Cuchullin."

"Never you are!" Oonah shrieked with surprise. "Did you see my Finn now?" she asked with grave concern.

"Never! He's always hidin', the skulkin' poltroon! I've never had the chance to trounce him."

"And lucky for you! If he ever sets eyes on you that will be the last of Cuchullin for sure now," warned Oonah, wide-eyed at the thought of Finn's fierceness. "I'm a peaceful woman myself, but I know as dust flies before the wind, Finn will deal with you, boyo. And speaking of the wind, there's such a creakin' at the door. Would you mind turning the house round now?"

"*Turn the house round*?" Cuchullin gasped.

"Please do. Finn always does it when he's home. It's just the sighin' of the mountain wind disturbin' the door and makin' it creak," Oonah explained. "Just turn the house out of the wind's path, that's all."

Cuchullin nodded and went out the door. *Crack-crack-crack*! Three times he cracked the middle finger of his right hand before he took hold of the house to wrench and heave, and heave and heave . . . until the house, creaking and swaying pivotted on its foundations to turn its back to the wind.

Oonah slid across the floor, so did the cradle, and under the quilt Finn shivered. Cuchullin's strength was indeed fearsome, and there was Oonah, as calm as a blue day, chatting through the door. "There! That wasn't hard now, was it? I'll be makin' some tea if you'll kindly fetch water from the spring. It's just there, under that little bit of rock by the path. Lovely water it is, but Finn says that he needs to pull the rock apart to free the spring. I doubt if he has the strength," she sighed. "It'll need two giants to break the stone loose."

Cuchullin took up a jug and shambled away to the spring, and very thoughtful he was. He didn't like what he was hearing about Finn. He liked less the huge, solid lump of mountain which blocked the spring. *Crack-crack-crack*! Three times he cracked the middle finger of his right hand before he took hold of the rock to lift and heave, and heave, and heave

. . . until it loosened, then rolled free. The spring gushed forth, a crystal-clear fountain of sparkling water flared and fell, tumbling and rushing in a torrent of foam and spray, pouring down the mountainside to become the river of sweet water which runs to this day.

The thunderous roar of the released water sent Finn worming deeper under his quilt and his nervous twitches rocked the cradle.

"Hush, you!" crooned Oonah and turned a smiling face to Cuchullin who was returning with the water jug. "Thank you kindly. Seat yourself by the fire and take a griddle-cake while the kettle boils for your tea," she invited him.

Twelve cakes piled the plate which she passed and Cuchullin was pleased to bite into one. *Crunch!* Two teeth, bigger than elephant's tusks, broke. Cuchullin howled. "What kind of a cake is this, Woman?"

"The cakes I bake for Finn. He never eats any other. I'm surprised that your teeth aren't stronger. Even little Finn can eat them. Try another! This one looks softer."

Cuchullin sniffed the cake suspiciously. It smelt spicy and vanilla-sweet as a cake should. He bit. *Crunch!* Two more teeth broke. He yelled. He spat. "Keep your cakes, Woman, or I'll not have a tooth in my head."

"Dear me!" flustered Oonah. "And hush! Keep that bellow down. You're frightening me babby."

Out of sight, under the quilt, Finn frantically sucked his thumb, then he opened his mouth and bawled, "*Wahhhhhhhh!*"

The great noise surprised Cuchullin. "Doth hith Dadda roar as louth ath that?" he asked through his broken teeth.

"I should say he does," said Oonah. "And what is Mumma's little lamb wanting?" she asked the lump in the

21

cradle. "Would me own darlin' like one of Mumma's cakes, now?" she wanted to know, taking up a cake with only currants and spice in its middle. "There! Put it into your mouthie and stop that weepin'."

Finn grabbed the cake. He gobbled it down, then roared for another, then another. Cuchullin watched in astonishment, watched the third cake disappear, then gulped, "I think I'll be leavin' now, Mithuth Finn. It'th a brave bonny lad you've got in that cradle."

"He is that," murmured Oonah proudly. "Look at his lovely strong legs now." She flipped back the blanket. Finn gurgled at her, kicking his legs in the air.

"That'th fine limbth on him, by golly!" exclaimed Cuchullin.

"Yes, he's growing nicely," purred Oonah. "At the same size, you know, his Dadda was out fightin' the bulls and boars in the bog. Still we can't expect everything. The babby has a fine set of teeth already."

"I believe that," agreed Cuchullin with great respect. "I juth thaw him eat three caketh, I did."

"So you *did* and you just should feel the babby's teeth now! Why don't you? You'll never set eyes on such a set again," urged Oonah, tugging Finn's thumb from his mouth and beckoning Cuchullin to step closer.

Slowly, gingerly he stretched out his right hand. Finn grabbed it. *Grind!* His teeth closed over Cuchullin's fingers.

Cuchullin screamed — wrenched back his hand. His middle finger, his strength finger was bitten off. He backed to the door whimpering, and Finn leapt from the cradle. *Wham!* He pitched a griddle-cake. It knocked Cuchullin down the

mountainside. He rolled away . . . *away* . . . *away* . . . *growing smaller and smaller until he was gone.*

Cuchullin was never seen there again, or anywhere else, and everyone was glad of that.

I WILL CATCH A GIANT

I will catch a giant By the toe, by the toe! I will catch a giant By the toe! Roar! Roar!

I will catch a troll
By the nose, by the nose!
I will catch a troll
By the nose! (TROLL NOISES)

I will catch an elf
By the ear, by the ear!
I will catch an elf
By the ear! (ELF SQUEAKS)

Finish the song. Find other creatures and animals to catch. It could become a collection of strange and spooky sounds. What would a ghost say? And where would you catch hold of a ghost?

SNEEZY SNATCHER

Once, long ago when strange things happened, Sam Small was a very bad, rotten aggravating nuisance — an absolute provoking puff-ball of a child. Over and over again people predicted, "Sneezy Snatcher will grab you one day, my lad. And don't say that you weren't warned!"

"Hoh! I'm not afraid of any old Sneezy Snatcher," boasted Sam. And he wasn't afraid — he wasn't afraid of anything. He went on being bad and awful, and one day, he nipped into the street where he should not have been. Sam Small peeked through a fence into a garden where some girls were skipping and chanting to the rhythm of the turning rope,

"Sneezy Snatcher, he will catch ya!
Boil you in a pot.
Sneezy Snatcher, stop your snoring,
How many boys have you got?
One . . . two, three-four-five-six . . ."

The skipping rope whirled faster and faster. The girls skipped and counted faster, faster, faster, and then one tripped. The rope jerked and stopped. "*Sixteen* boys!" they shrilled, and their game of Peppers started over again.

"Yah! Sneezy Snatcher is only a silly old skipping game!" scoffed Sam Small. "There's no such person as Sneezy Snatcher."

"Isn't there now?" thundered a great bottomless voice. It cracked through the air like gunfire. Sam's ears rang with the din of it and, before he could protect them with his hands, he was snatched off the ground in a sickening swiftness, yanked upwards to dingle-dangle like an apple on a branch. Next thing, he could see nothing but blueness which was as bright

as a bauble and as round as a cooking pot. Sam stared into the
unblinking eye of a giant. He yelped. Then he kicked and
struggled, twisting and untwisting in dizzy swirls from his
shirt-tail which was held fast between Sneezy Snatcher's
fore-finger and thumb.

Whump! Sneezy dropped Sam into a sack. He bottomed like
a pumpkin then pitched forwards as Sneezy hoisted the sack to
his shoulder and tramped away to goodness-knows-where.

Sam screeched, hating the dark mustiness enclosing him,
loathing its floury smell, and queasy from lumping, bumping
and flinging about with each jarring stride of the giant.

Just when he thought every breath was knocked from him
Sam toppled from the sack to land with a thud on Sneezy's
kitchen table.

"Are you a fat boy or a skinny boy?" Sneezy wanted to know with a pinch and a poke at Sam.

"Skinny! What a shame! He's a skinny one!" sighed Butterball, Sneezy's dumpling-round wife.

"Then you'll have to boil him," regretted Sneezy who loved roast dinners best of all.

"And I'll have to boil him for a long time," Butterball sighed as she prodded Sam's ribs. "Fetch me some herbs for the pot, Sneezy. Lots of them! Otherwise he won't taste well. Parsley and rosemary, mace, thyme and sage, lots of onions, too!"

Sneezy tramped out of the kitchen and Butterball smiled down at Sam. A sweet-tempered, mild kind of smile. A round-cheeked, dimpling smile. "He won't be long," she said.

Quick as quick, Sam scrambled to his feet and shouted to Butterball, "Does Sneezy Snatcher always eat boys for dinner?"

"Aye! When he can catch them. Boys are hard to catch."

"Does he eat vegetables as well?"

"Aye! Sneezy eats vegetables when he can get them."

"And pudding? Does he eat pudding?"

"Aye! Sneezy dearly loves a bit of puddin' when he can get it. Puddin' is hard to get. Times are bad and Sneezy does love puddin'. I wish I had one for him," Butterball mourned.

"My mother made a great puddin' this morning," recalled Sam Small. "It's full of eggs and butter and apples."

"Mmmmmm! I wish I could taste that!" drooled Butterball.

"There's enough of it, I should think," bragged Sam. "As big as my head it was! And there's cinnamon and nutmeg and raisins in it."

"Cinnamon, nutmeg and raisins!" groaned Butterball.

"And *almonds*!"

28

Butterball's eyes rolled to look at the ceiling. "Don't talk of it," she begged. "It makes my mouth fair water."

"We'll eat it with custard and cream."

"Custard and cream as well!" Butterball rocked with delight, remembering the smooth taste of custard and cream.

"My Ma would give you a slice or two, and a dribble of custard, and a dollop of cream," piped Sam. "Why don't I run home and ask for some puddin' for you?"

"Oh, would you? Would you do that? Sneezy does love puddin'!" dimpled Butterball.

"I'll run like the wind," promised Sam.

"Do that, Laddie. Be back in good time to be boiled."

Zerp! Sam was off — home in no time. And did his Ma send him back with slices of pudding for Sneezy Snatcher's dinner? Certainly not! Her pudding was not big enough to share with giants, and she did *not* have a pot big enough to make another giant-sized one.

Sneezy Snatcher and Butterball would still be waiting for their pudding, except that giants left that place long ago.

GIANT-SIZED PICTURES AND MURALS

Make a giant-sized poster of yourself or your friends. You will need to sticky-tape or glue together lots of sheets of newspaper.

Ask the tallest person you know to lie flat out on the paper. Use chalk to draw round the person's shape.

Now the shape can be painted. You may like to use one colour only, or to paint clothes on your giant. Let it dry.

Carefully cut round the shape. Hang it on a wall or a door.

Several people can work together to make a long, wide mural. Again you will need to sticky-tape or glue together as many sheets of newspaper as you think you'll need. Secure the paper to a wall. You'll need help for sure.

Everyone paints or draws whatever each one fancies. Or everyone can share in the same idea. A gigantic town scene maybe. An adventure in space perhaps.

Crayons, chalks, inks and anything else which marks can be used.

For interesting textures paste or pin to the mural paper or materials, cotton-wool or string, foil, lace, anything at all if it looks well.

Sometimes a mural can be painted straight on to a wall, even the four walls of an old shed, or room. However, ask your grown-ups first. Also ask if you may use water-proof paints, if you want the mural to last.

NICHT NOUGHT NOTHING

Once, a King and Queen who had been long married, were blessed with a son. At the time of the Prince's birth the King was far away at a war, and his Queen did not name her babe. "We'll just call him Nicht Nought Nothing until my Lord returns," she told the court. "The King must name his child." And strange as it sounds, Nicht Nought Nothing he was called until he grew from baby to toddler, from toddler to noisy little boy.

By then, at long last, the King was returning home. His journey brought him to a river which ran wide and wild, in full flood. The King rode along the bank seeking a safe place to cross, but he found no shallows and the currents were too strong to swim his horse. He had to wait until the river fell.

As he dismounted, the ground shuddered. Then the trees swayed, shaking their boughs and shedding twigs. Above the river's roar grew a strange rumbling. It rumbled louder and closer until . . . until above the tree-tops a Giant grinned down on him. "What will you give me, King, if I carry you over the river?" he boomed.

The King, trying to conceal his shock, shouted back, "What is in my power to give you, Sir?"

"Awh! What about Nicht Nought Nuttin'?"

"Come now! Nicht Nought Nothing is too little payment for your service, Sir. I shall give you my thanks as well."

"Done!" droned the Giant. Little did the King know that he had unwittingly promised his small son to the Evil One.

With the King high on his shoulder the Giant lurched across the river. "Don't forget! You promised me Nicht Nought Nuttin'," he reminded the King, as he dumped His Majesty on the bank. "Should you forget, I will destroy your kingdom, your people and you!" he threatened.

"I'll remember," nodded the King, believing the Giant was soft in the head. The Big Buffoon's threats were absurd moonshine twaddle as foolish as his thick-skulled demand for Nicht Nought Nothing. Pish and fiddle-de-dee!

Hours later the King's home-coming turned to sorrow and despair. His own son was Nicht Nought Nothing! "What have I done?" he moaned. "What have I done?"

"Take heart! We shall *never* give our boy to the Giant," vowed the Queen.

Next morning, leering with malice, the Giant bent over the castle wall, and bellowed for his reward. He was given a boy, the Henwife's lad who was carried off, shoulder-high.

They jogged along and jogged along until they came to a rock which was large enough for the Giant to sit on, and as he eased out his long bulky legs, he asked,

"Hidge-hodge on my back,
What's the time now?
Tell me that!"

"It's the time my mother takes the eggs to the castle for the Queen's breakfast," piped up the Henwife's lad.

"*Arrrrrh!*" The Giant was enraged. He dropped the boy. Roaring, thundering, punching at the air he stamped back to the castle. "Give me Nicht Nought Nuttin'!" he bellowed. And he was given a boy, the Gardener's lad, who was carried off, shoulder-high.

They trotted along and trotted along until they came to a rock which was large enough for the Giant to sit on.

"Hidge-hodge on my back,

What's the time now? Tell me that!" he rumbled.

"It's the time when my father cuts cabbages for the Queen's dinner," answered the Gardener's lad.

"*Orrrh!*" The Giant was livid. He dropped the lad. He raged. Pulling up trees, pitching rocks, kicking at hillsides, stomping on barns, he boiled back to the castle to shake its tower and thunder, "Trick me again, King-in-the-castle, and I will destroy your house, your people, your kingdom and your Nicht Nought Nuttin'."

Nicht Nought Nothing yelled back. "Here I am, Giant. Take me!" And the Giant had him up, on his back like a bag of chaff before the Queen could grab her child's coat-tails.

They travelled fast, travelled until the sun was setting and the Giant asked,

"Hidge-hodge on my back,

What's the time now? Tell me that!"

"It must be time for my father, the King, to sit at his supper," answered Nicht Nought Nothing.

"Then the King has given me his promise," guffawed the Giant.

They travelled faster now, on to the Land of Giants where the Prince was to grow from boy to man. During those years of imprisonment his only friend was the Giant's daughter, and the Old Dunderhead never realised how fond they were of

each other. When at last he twigged that his Gillyflower and the Prince were friends he fumed and raged. He planned to be rid of the impertinent, lickspittle of a prince. "I've a stable seven miles long and seven miles wide. It's not been cleaned for seven years. Clean it by sunset tomorrow or, Nicht Nought Nuttin', I'll have you for my supper."

The Prince surely would have been stewed or roasted if Gilly, small and fragile as her flower name, hadn't brewed a spell. Animals, small and large from thereabouts, flocked to her, and clouds of birds flew from the sky. "Please clean the stable before my Papa comes home!" she begged.

Animals scratched and dug and carried. Birds pecked and picked and carried. By sunset the stable was clean and the Giant purple with fury. "Shame on the clever one who has helped you!" he ranted. "And don't think I've done with you yet. Tomorrow you will drain the castle's lake, or I'll eat you for supper, Nicht Nought Nuttin'!"

The lake was seven miles long and seven miles wide and seven miles deep. Water lapped its shores, and although the Prince worked digging drains and channels, the lake stayed brim-full. It was a hopeless task until Gilly chanted a charm which brought the fish from the sea — flapping, slithering, flicking fish, flying through the air. "Please drink the lake dry before my Papa comes home," begged Gilly.

Swallowing, gulping, gurgling fish drained the lake.

"Shame on the one who helped you!" raged the Giant. "And don't think I've done with you yet. Tomorrow, Nicht Nought Nuttin' you will bring me the egg from the nest that rests on the top of the pine trees, seven miles high. Otherwise I'll be eating you with bread and butter for supper."

Alas, Gilly knew no other spells or charms. There was only one way she could help the Prince. She used her fingers and

36

toes as a ladder for Nicht Nought Nothing to scale the tree. He took the egg but as he slithered down it cracked, cracked inside his shirt.

"Somehow we must escape before Papa returns," said Gilly and leaving the egg on the giant's table she snatched up a magical flask which she clutched in both hands and they ran and they ran.

Too soon the Giant pursued them — his long earth-rocking strides bringing him close.

"Take the pin from my hair," Gilly told Nicht Nought Nothing. "Cast it down behind us."

The Prince threw down the pin and wonders upon wonders, a river flowed between them and the Giant!

They ran farther, but too soon the Giant crossed the river. Too soon, they heard his pounding feet.

"Take the comb from my hair and cast it behind us," Gilly cried out.

Nicht Nought Nothing threw down the comb. At once a hedge, bristling with thorns, sprang up between them and the Giant.

They ran much farther, but too soon the Giant plunged through the hedge and too soon, his heavy breathing was like a hot wind on their backs.

Gilly turned. She threw down the flask. It broke into a hundred gleaming crystals of diamond-bright glass, and from the crystals rose a foaming water wave which arched over the Giant, engulfing him, swirling him, drowning him.

Gilly, shocked and exhausted, could not travel on. Nicht Nought Nothing went ahead alone to find them shelter. Soon he came to a castle standing behind walls of a great height, and there, tired to his very bones, the Prince fell wearily asleep in a chair near the door to the great hall.

The castle folk gathered about him, inspecting and guessing that he could only be a foreign prince. And the Gardener's daughter sidled up to peep, and admire. She was vastly annoyed when the Cook sent her to fetch water from the well.

By this time Gilly had entered the castle grounds. She heard the stomping footsteps and the clanking bucket as the girl neared the well. Gilly fled, into the nearby tree, clinging to a bough, fearful that the angry girl would discover her refuge.

The Gardener's daughter did glimpse Gilly's reflection. Her pale face, framed in leaves, shone as if from a mirror in the water below her. "Glory be!" sighed the Gardener's daughter. "It's lovely and beautiful I am, and I never did know it!" She dropped her bucket. "What am I, a lovely-lovely, doin' here at the well? I'll be up to the castle and marry that Prince." She flounced away, tripping lightly with toes turned out and bottom waggling, and her nose tipped up in the air.

The Gardener discovered his daughter in her conceited state when the Cook shouted for water, so he went to the well himself. He too, gazed upon Gilly's reflection. "Hey, you! Come down from there!" he ordered her. "*You*, rickety old hag, have bewitched my daughter!"

Gilly scrambled from the tree and the Gardener saw that she was a frightened weary girl, trying hard not to weep. "Now then, a tree's no place for a lady, Ma'am!" he said, offering her his arm. "I'll take you to the Queen."

As they entered the castle hall Gilly pulled away to fling herself at the Prince's feet. "Wake! Speak to me!" she whispered, taking his hands and kissing them, wetting them with her tears.

The castle folk gawked, then shuffled aside unwillingly to admit the Queen, and then the King, who heard Gilly sob,

"I cleared the stable,
I drained the lake,
I climbed the tree
For love of thee.
Wilt thou now awake
And speak to me?
Speak to me!"

She pressed his hands against her cheek and looked at the Queen in anguish. "Nicht Nought Nothing cannot speak to me."

"Nicht Nought Nothing!" repeated the Queen faintly, pale and astonished.

"*My son!*" shouted the King, clutching the Queen.

They thrust Gilly aside. The Queen snatched Nicht Nought Nothing into her arms and rocked him. He woke bewildered, looking about wildly, struggling to escape, until his eyes met Gilly's and he smiled with joy.

It was a long time before the excitement simmered down and stories were exchanged. There was never any doubt that Nicht Nought Nothing was safely home. The grateful King and elated Queen wanted nothing more than Gillyflower to live with them as their daughter.

Nicht Nought Nothing wanted nothing more than Gilly to marry him, which she did in due course, and everyone lived happily for the rest of their lives.

OGRE MASK

An ogre, as big as any giant and twice as ugly,
was a blood-thirsty people-hater.
Make an ogre mask as ugly, as fearsome, as
hideous as you can.
You will need:
    1 round balloon
    string
    lots of newspaper
    tissue paper
    wallpaper paste
    paint
    egg-carton cups
    knife
    scissors
    1 grown-up

Blow up the balloon.
If possible suspend it over the work-table.
It will be easier to work on if it is hung.
Now tear lots of strips from the newspaper.
Paste them over the balloon.
Cover the balloon evenly.
Let the strips dry. Paste on another layer.
You will need at least four layers of paper.
Let the balloon dry out.

Ask an adult to slice it in half.
You will have two masks needing noses.
Paste on an egg-carton cup. Two would make
a bumpy-lump of a nose.
Or use a paper cup.
Mark places for the eyes.
The grown-up can cut out the eyes.
It's hard work.
Cover the mask with a layer of tissue paper.
Paint a hideous face.
You can use wool for eyebrows and hair, or
decorate your masks in your own way.
Attach elastic — the very thin kind — at about
ear height each side.

Better still, with adult help, poke a piece of
dowel under the chin to make a handle. Hold
the mask before your face and off you go,
Scary One.
Be sure that the handle is firm.

TIMIMOTO AND THE SILVER NEEDLE-SWORD

Timimoto was not much bigger than your thumb. He ate from a nutshell. He slept in a rice bowl. He rode in his father's pocket to see the village. He dangled from his mother's ear to see the river. And that's where he was, swinging like an earring when they took the washing to the river bank one morning.

"Mother, it's time that I went off to see the world," Timimoto told her.

She wept and cried out. "My son, you are so small! People will trample you. Stay at home with your father and me."

No, he must go, and that evening he sailed away in a rice-bowl boat, using chopsticks as oars. His mother's parting gift was a silver needle, a long slim needle as sharp as a sword.

Down the river . . . and down the river sped the rice bowl. The hungry bulging eyes of a frog saw it swirl by. The frog sprang, open-mouthed, ready to swallow Timimoto in a gulp. *Swish!* He lunged. The silver needle-sword punctured the frog. It tumbled backwards into the river and floated away.

Down the river . . . and down the river sped the rice bowl,

to be washed ashore where a city dipped its streets into the shallows as if to wash its grimy feet.

Timimoto beached his boat and jumped ashore, ready to explore, ready for adventure.

People crowded the streets. Timimoto ducked and dodged, side-stepped and scuttled, skittered and jumped from the dangers of shuffling sandals and tramping boots. Then, as a crushing foot loomed alarmingly close, he sprang to the safety of the closest wheel on a passing ox cart. He clung to the hub, jolted and shaken, until at last the cart came to a stop.

"Thanks for the ride!" he trilled to the Driver. His tiny voice sounded like the chirrup of a cricket, and the man who glanced about with interest tried to locate the sound.

"I'm down here. Look at your toe!" shouted Timimoto. The Driver saw him now. Slowly, gently, carefully, he lifted Timimoto from the ground. Slowly, he balanced him on the lined palm of his old hand, looked at him in amazement, then said, "Whoever you are, Little One, you had best be getting home."

"But I've only just left home to see the world," explained Timimoto.

"Then find a safe crack where you can hide. As soon as the sun goes down a great monster, the Ogre and none other, will walk the streets. Whoever he finds he *eats*!"

"I'm not afraid of the Ogre."

"I am!" The Driver bowed his farewell and drove away, rattling and bouncing the cart in his haste.

Timimoto looked about and saw that the streets were emptying fast, as people hurried into doorways like scuttling beetles. When the sun dipped out of the sky the streets were suddenly silent. Everyone had fled.

"Well, I'm here and here I'll stay," Timimoto shrugged. "Besides, I've never seen an Ogre."

"Who has never seen an Ogre?"

"The Great and Honourable Timimoto, and whatever Timimoto says is the truth!"

"Then Timimoto has spoken the truth for the last time!" snarled the Ogre lunging from the shadows. His sword whistled. He swung and struck downwards. *Crash!* He missed Timimoto and his blade scored the pavement. Timimoto, nimble as a fly, flicked from the sword's path. Again it sliced the earth. Then the Ogre smote low, swinging the sword in slashing, widening arcs; each swipe closer to the ground . . . once, twice, ten, twenty times.

But Timimoto had already sprung away to the Ogre's foot, then jumped to a bent knee, flipped to an elbow, then shoulder, and with a great leap to his head, where he perched astride the Ogre's helmet. And he clung there while the Ogre slashed and hewed, chopped and sliced at his invisible enemy.

Little by little Timimoto pulled the silver needle-sword from his belt, then with his greatest strength he thrust it down, deep between the Ogre's eyes.

The monster roared. He reeled with pain. He crashed to the road and Timimoto fell with him, gripping the metal rim of the helmet. A great blast of air, the Ogre's dying breath, blew Timimoto clear of the mountainous body.

"No one need be afraid of the Ogre again!" Timimoto shouted, then searched about for his silver needle-sword. It was very troublesome to see and when his eye did discover its glinting slimness, Timimoto gasped. It was shrinking, shrinking smaller and smaller. "Mercy me! It's almost too small to pick up!"

It was not the needle-sword which had dwindled in size. It was the same length and the same thickness. For the first time in many years, Timimoto was growing — upwards and outwards. His bones lengthened, his chest expanded to those of a six-year-old boy's, then a twelve-year-old lad's, a fourteen-year-old youth's, a twenty-year-old man's.

"Stop! Stop!" Timimoto clapped his hand on the top of his head. "I don't want to be ogre-high!" But maybe he would have been, had not the Ogre sighed his last breath when Timimoto was just a finger-nail taller than the men in that city, no more.

People poured out now, hurrying from houses and corners to congratulate him. They wanted him to stay as their Lord, but Timimoto was thinking fondly of his home. He stayed long enough to help clean out the Ogre's cave which was a store of stolen treasure.

Timimoto departed with a cart-load of gold and jewels to share with his people, but his most treasured possession was the silver needle-sword. It had slain the Ogre and released the strange power of magical growth which had been spell-bound in the Ogre's breath.

45

I'M NOT AFRAID

Are you afraid of any monster? Never!
Think of other things a monster might do.
Here are some to add to your own ideas... whistling,
buzzing, sneezing, humming, finger clicking, mouth
popping, kissing.
And here's one way to end the song:

I'm not afraid of the nothing monster,
I'm not afraid at all.
I'm not afraid of the nothing monster,
I'm not afraid at all.
And it goes (SILENCE)
And it goes (SILENCE)

HEY-HOW FOR HALLOWE'EN!

Hey-how for Hallowe'en!
A' the witches tae be seen,
Some are black, an' some green,
Hey-how for Hallowe'en.

HALLOWE'EN

If you say *All Hallow's Eve* often and very quickly as if it were a tongue-twister, it shortens to *Hallowe'en*. Hallowe'en falls on 31st October, the day before All Saints' Day on 1st November.

Long ages ago, people believed that Hallowe'en was when restless spirits, awesome ghosts and other spine-tingling creatures were abroad. Witches flew, and fairy courts moved to their winter quarters. All could be sent skulking back to their haunts by loud rackety noise and the leaping flames of bonfires.

One way and another, for many it was a special time of the year, and some of the best customs are still celebrated, although no one still believes in the Old Horribles, except in stories.

CHARM AGAINST WITCHES

Bring the holy crust of bread,
Lay it underneath the head:
'tis a certain charme to keep
Hags away, while children sleep.
Robert Herrick

BABA YAGA'S SEVEN SWAN-GEESE

Once, and long ago it was, Katya was left to mind her fat baby brother while her parents went to sow the fields. She put the baby down on the grass and ran off to chat with her friends.

No sooner had Katya left than a flock of swan-geese, seven great white birds, swooped from the skies and carried off the little boy.

Katya heard his squeals and at first, she didn't know what to do. She ran about weeping and calling and searching for her brother, but he was nowhere. Then, far away, where the sky and fields met, she saw the swan-geese strung across the blueness like a strand of thick white wool. She knew then what had become of her brother. The swan-geese had stolen him.

Watching the birds and stumbling across the fields of newly tilled earth, she followed their flight. She ran until she was breathless. Then the birds dropped from sight below the horizon and Katya bumped into an oven. An oven in a field? She was too distressed to be amazed and cried out, "Oven! Please, Oven, tell me where the swan-geese have flown."

"Eat one of my rye loaves, then I shall tell what I know," answered the oven.

"I couldn't do that! At my father's house I only eat fine wheaten loaves, never black bread. Besides I must find my brother." Katya was too distracted to be mindful of the oven's request.

She ran on, out of the field to an apple tree growing at the meadow's edge. "Apple Tree! Please, Apple Tree, tell me where the swan-geese have flown."

"Eat one of my wild apples, then I shall tell what I know," answered the apple tree.

"I couldn't do that! At my father's house I only eat garden-sweet apples. Besides I must find my brother."

Katya ran faster over the meadow's springy green grass and she met a cow. "Cow! Please, Cow, tell me where the swan-geese have flown."

"Drink some of my sour milk, then I shall tell what I know."

"I couldn't do that! At my father's house I only drink fresh sweet milk. Besides I must find my brother."

Once more Katya ran. She ran into darkness, thick and shadowy, through which a light flashed from the window of a hut, a vile eyesore of a place which perched high off the ground, a-top four clawed chicken legs. Slowly, eerily the hut circled round and round, flashing the swinging light. It lit up Baba Yaga, another vile eyesore — bone-thin hooked nose and long pointed chin; glinting, never-still frog-eyes forever rolling, forever spying and prying; greedy mouth, thick of lips and dribblesome; and hair streaked and bristling like a deserted bird's nest. Oh, she was something to see and there

she sat spinning and in need of a scrubbing and combing. At her feet sat Katya's little brother, playing with five silver balls!

Katya's heart leaped with joy, then thudded with fear. "Good evening, Granny!" she called. Oh, she was much braver than she felt.

"Now what brings you here, Little One?" cackled Baba Yaga, hobbling to the door.

"My dress is wet with dew. May I dry it by your fire?" Katya asked primly, never mentioning her brother. She knew that the old witch would enchant them both if she were crossed in any way.

"Dry your dress, you shall," honeyed Baba Yaga showing her long green and yellow teeth. "Come to the fire and I'll fetch water to make you some tea." She handed her spindle to Katya, then sprang from the door, calling, "Spin for me, Child, while I'm gone."

Katya began to spin as if she couldn't stop. Her brother played as if he couldn't stop. And there they were half-bewitched in the still quiet hut when a mouse crept from its hole under the stove. "Give me some porridge, Katya! There! From the pot on the stove," it squeaked.

"Of course!" she said and spooned out porridge for the mouse.

As the mouse ate it said, "Baba Yaga is in the bath-house, Katya. She is boiling water in the copper, Katya, to steam you and wash you, then roast you in the oven, Katya. She will eat you up, then ride the sky on your bones, Katya!"

Katya almost fainted and only just heard the mouse advise, "Put your brother on your hip, Katya, and run for home. I will spin tow for you."

In a daze, Katya picked up her brother, jumped from the hut and sped away.

From the bath-house Baba Yaga screamed, "Are you spinning, dear Child?"

"I am spinning, Granny!" shrieked the mouse.

Nodding her head, licking her lips, Baba Yaga stoked the fire and the copper bubbled and steamed. She clanged on its lid, sprang into the house and found her prize was gone. And the fat boy-babe! And the mouse . . . into its hole. The spindle lay on the floor in a tangle of tow.

"*Eeeeee!*" Baba Yaga squawked. "Swan-geese, fly! Capture Katya! Capture the boy! Swan-geese, Fly!"

Wings flapped and seven wildly honking swan-geese flew, flew low, seeking Katya. She heard their beating wings and called across the meadow, "Help me, please, Cow!"

"Drink some of my sour milk," said the cow.

Katya swallowed a choking, cloying, sour mouthful, then another and another, and the cow nudged the children down beside her, hiding them in her bulky shadow as the swan-geese winged overhead unable to see their prey.

Now Katya ran to the apple tree, but the swan-geese swerved, doubling-back towards her. "Help me, please, Apple Tree!" she begged.

"Eat one of my wild apples."

Katya chewed into the bitter apple, crunching, shuddering, swallowing mouthfuls as the apple tree stooped, spreading out leafy branches which covered the children like sheltering arms, and once more, the swan-geese missed their prey.

And once more Katya ran on. Her arms ached with the weight of her brother. Her legs slowed with pain. A stitch stabbed sharply at her side. Somehow, she limped on but the swan-geese honked, screamed and screeched above her head.

Katya made for the oven. "Please, oh please, help me!"

"Eat one of my loaves."

Gasping, Katya bit into the crusted, dusty-dry, dark loaf. It cut and scratched her mouth, but she swallowed mouthful after mouthful, and the oven pushed the children through its door and clanged it shut.

Katya heard the swan-geese screaming, thrashing the oven with their wings, clawing and pecking it, bullying it to give up the children. And they attacked the oven until at last Baba Yaga whistled them home.

Katya tumbled out of the oven and carried her little brother to their house. No sooner were they settled inside than their parents came in with hugs and kisses for the children. Then there were pancakes with sugar and cream for supper.

As for Baba Yaga, she went without supper and no doubt is still hungry, because swan-geese gave up stealing children long, long ago.

OLD WITCH, OLD WITCH!

It didn't need to be Hallowe'en for old Baba Yaga to ride the night skies. She flew when it suited her in a mortar and pestle. The old witch's favourite haunts were the mountain-tops of Russia, Poland and Czechoslovakia.

The Hickory-stick Witch lived in America where her song was first sung by children. Now you can share it. Sing it at any time, not only at Hallowe'en.

Chick - en my chick - en my cream - y crow, I

went to the well to wash my toe,

When I got there the wa - ter was low,

What time is it, Old Witch, Old Witch?

What time is it Old Witch? Old

Witch, Old Witch, she lives in a ditch, And

combs her hair with a hick-o-ry switch. She

lives on nails and snails and flies And

if you go near she'll wob-ble her eyes,

Oh, she'll wob-ble her eyes,

Oh, she'll wob-ble her eyes.

Chicken my chicken my creamy cran,
I went to the well to wash my hand,
When I got there the water was sand,
What time is it, Old Witch, Old Witch?
What time is it, Old Witch?

Old Witch, Old Witch, she lives in a ditch
And combs her hair with a hickory switch,
She's fat as a feather but tight in the middle
And when she talks she sounds like a fiddle.
Oh, she sounds like a fiddle!
Oh, she sounds like a fiddle!

Chicken my chicken my creamy crase,
I went to the well to wash my face,
But when I got there the water was lace,
What time is it, Old Witch, Old Witch?
What time is it, Old Witch?

Old Witch, Old Witch, she lives in a ditch
And combs her hair with a hickory switch.
She sleeps on a bed with straw and corn
And when she snores she sounds like a horn,
Oh she sounds like a horn!
She sounds like a horn!

Chicken my chicken my creamy cregs,
I went to the well to wash my legs,
And when I got there the water was dregs,
What time is it, Old Witch, Old Witch?
What time is it, Old Witch?

Old Witch, Old Witch, she lives in a ditch.
And combs her hair with a hickory switch.
And as I said she's very fat
And when she walks she jumps like a cat,
Oh, she jumps like a cat!
Oh, she jumps like a cat!

GUISERS

For more years than anyone has bothered to count, as soon as it's dark at Hallowe'en, out come the *Guisers*. In Europe and North America and some parts of Australia, children carry on the old custom of disguising themselves in fancy dress, or over-large clothes. They blacken their faces with soot, or paint them weirdly with make-up. No one is supposed to recognize them, and away they go, rattling on windows, knocking on doors and shouting, "Trick or treat!" Often they are both tricked and treated.

Here are a few Guiser disguises:

Beard

Cut a strip of coloured crepe paper about 23 cm by 30 cm. Fold it in half *length-wise*. Cut the edges into a fringe. *Do not cut the fold*.
The fringe can be curled by rolling each piece with a knitting needle.
Trim the beard to a shape you like.
Fasten it to your hair with hair-slides, or an elastic hair-band.

Moustache

Fold a piece of stiff paper about 10 cm by 20 cm in half *side-wise*.
Draw the shape you fancy. Colour it, then cut it out.
Fasten to your upper lip with sticky tape.

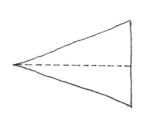

Sticky-beak Nose

From stiff paper cut a triangle with a base about 12 cm and as long as you like. Fold it down the centre, creasing it well. Paint it. Attach it to your nose with tape.

Lump-and-a-bump of a nose

Glue, or sticky-tape together two cups from an egg carton. Decorate it and tape over your own nose.

Masks

Measure the width and height of your forehead.

Cut a strip of light cardboard to fit the measurement.

Fold it in half.

Draw on whatever pattern you like. Mark the position of the wearer's eyes very accurately — you may need help with this.

Cut out the mask. Do not cut the fold — you'll have two pieces and you only need one. Cut out the eyes.

Decorate the mask with paint, crayons, feathers, spangles, flowers, streamers, anything at all.

Glue one end to a piece of dowelling as a handle, or attach some hat elastic to keep it on your head.

Guisers often carry a turnip lantern, an apple candle, a Jack o' lantern, or a torch with the glass covered in coloured cellophane to make a dim spooky light. Try shining the torch directly up under your chin. Very, very scary!

Turnip lantern

With someone to help, slice the top off a fat turnip, then scrape out enough flesh to firmly hold a candle. A few dribbles of wax in the hollow will help to fasten the candle.
BE VERY CAREFUL NOT TO BURN YOURSELF, SOMEONE ELSE OR ANYTHING. FIRST, ASK PERMISSION FROM YOUR ADULT BEFORE LIGHTING A CANDLE.

Apple Candle

Slice a piece off the bottom so the apple can stand evenly. Remove the core from the apple and push a slim candle into the space.

Jack o' lantern

Cut the top off a pumpkin. Hollow out the seeds and flesh. Ask a grown-up to cut out a face. Put a candle, or a torch inside the pumpkin. It makes a good decoration for a party.

62

THE SORCERER'S APPRENTICE

Once a lad chanced to meet a tall man so stooped with age that he was as bent as the stick he leaned upon. "Where are you going, Boy?" he asked.

"To seek my fortune," said the lad.

"Then, perhaps you could work for me. But first, tell me, can you read?"

"Can I read? My Lord! I can read better than the school master, the doctor and the village priest. Yes, I can!"

"Then, alas, you will be of no use to me," regretted the old man, shuffling away, tortoise-slow and ruefully watched by the boy.

However, as soon as the old chap crept about the corner, the boy swirled around, jumped into the air, clicked his heels, clicked his fingers and whooped. Almost before his feet hit the ground again he was pulling off his jacket. One wriggle and a shove and a thrust and it was returned to his back, but inside out. *Slappity-slap!* He brushed his hair down over his eyes, then raced off across the fields.

Some distance on, he rejoined the road, where he lolled by a tree to await the appearance of the old gentleman. Sure enough, he toddled into sight. "Good morning, Sir! Could you tell me if I could get work in these parts?" he called out in greeting.

"You could perhaps work for me. But first, young man, can you read?"

"Not a word!" lied the lad, hanging his head in regret.

"You're the lad I need," he was told. "Come along with me. It's good food that you'll have. A warm bed and a silver shilling each week."

And so the boy took service with a Sorcerer, becoming his apprentice.

Every day the Apprentice washed the flasks and scrubbed the cauldron. He cleaned the shelves. He swept floors and sorted the herbs. He filled some bottles and emptied others. He dusted rows and rows of books which he read whenever he was out of the Sorcerer's sight. It wasn't long before the hoodwinking young bluffer thought he knew as much about spells and magic as the Sorcerer had taken a life-time to learn. If only he could test his skill . . . if only . . . if only!

The chance came on the day the Sorcerer said, "Amuse yourself this morning, Boy. I'll be away for an hour on business at the court."

Hurray! The Apprentice whistled with delight, and no sooner had the Sorcerer left than he was draping his birch broom in an old cloak. Mutter-mutter-gibble-gabble! He chanted a spell. Presto! Marvello! The broom became a man, a broom-man with arms and legs like sticks and a shock of stiff ungroomed hair.

"Go to the well and fetch water for my bath," ordered the Apprentice.

"I obey!" rasped the Broom-man. He bent. He straightened, swinging a bucket in each hand. He marched straight-backed like a stake to the well. He drew the water, stepped back to the house and stalked down the stairs as stiff-legged as a crane from the marsh.

Water sploshed from the buckets to the bath. Then, up the stairs, out of the house, over the courtyard to the well stumped the Broom-man. Back to the bath! *Splash!* Back to the well! Back to the bath! *Splash!* Back to the well!

The Broom-man worked without a pause. He filled the bath to overflowing. Dribbling water puddled the floor. The puddle spread into a pool. Then the tiles were awash and a little stream trickled to the hall. "Stop! That's enough!" yelled the Apprentice. "Stop! I told you to stop!"

The Broom-man worked on. In with full buckets! Out with empty buckets! In! Out! In! Out! "Stop! *Stop!*" screamed the Apprentice. Soon the Broom-man was knee-deep in water, then thigh-deep, then waist-deep, then neck-deep in sloshing, rocking cold-cold water. Behind him gabbled the Apprentice repeating every spell he could remember. Each was useless.

He blocked the Broom-man's path. He stood astride with out-stretched arms, but the Broom-man swung him aside, marched on, down the stairs, under the water to the bath.

In with full buckets! Out with empty buckets! In! Out! In! Out! Like a tide the water rose up the stairs and flooded into the hall. Down the stairs, under the water continued the Broom-man. In! Out!

Miffed and flustered, the Apprentice grabbed the buckets as the Broom-man passed. He tugged. On strode the Broom-man dragging the Apprentice with him. Down the stairs! Under the water!

Spluttering, he released the buckets and fuming with anger

the boy fetched an axe and rashly struck downwards, through the Broom-man's head. It split in halves. Each piece was a new Broom-man. Each Broom-man carried two pails. Each bucket was filled with water. *Whack! Chip-chop! Chop-chop-chop!* The Apprentice split and gashed, surrounded himself with wood splinters. And up rose six, then twelve, twenty-four; a line of Broom-men filling and emptying buckets.

Water poured into the bedrooms, the kitchen, the Sorcerer's workshop. Half-swimming, half-wading, the frantic Apprentice fought the water to reach the shelves of great books and with trembling fingers he searched the pages for the right words to break the broom-stick spell.

All at once, large and fearsome, the Sorcerer stood in the doorway. The Apprentice slammed shut the book. The Sorcerer slammed the workshop door.

The boy stood there for a long time, hearing nothing except his beating heart, then the draining of water, rushing and gurgling away. He believed he was imprisoned but when he slunk to the door it opened at his touch.

The water was gone and only the broom's remains littered the tiles, in a heap of snapped birch twigs and harmless splinters of wood. Two upturned buckets drained by the well, leaving a shallow puddle of water which soon dried in the sun.

There was no sign of the Sorcerer, so the Apprentice, with his hands in his pockets, swaggered down the road, whistling. Some say he later became a successful plumber and invented plug-holes with drains, a big improvement upon the Sorcerer's solid stone bath. And he was never to utter that charm, or any other as long as he lived. Never! He never knew how to undo the broom-stick spell. The Sorcerer magicked away the great books, which was very prudent of him.

INVISIBLE MESSAGE

Some children have a party at Hallowe'en. Should you have friends at your house, send an invisible invitation — a secret one which only the receiver can read.

Cut some paper into a fancy shape. Perhaps a witch's hat, a cat, a pumpkin, even an owl.

Soak it in water until it is soggy, not too wet, or it'll fall to pieces. Lay the paper on a mirror.

Write the message with the point of a knitting needle, or a biro which no longer writes. Leave the paper to dry.

It should look blank until held up to the light to read the message. The receiver needs to know that, too.

TRICKS AND TEASERS

Hallowe'en tricks and teasers can be anything you like, but here are some old games which are still played.

Apple Duck
You need a bucket or tub with apples floating in water.
The players' hands are tied behind their backs.
They kneel before the tub trying to capture an apple in their teeth.
Sometimes a fork is held between the teeth to spear an apple.
Let the grown-ups play that way.
A coin can be dropped into the tub instead of the apples.
Use less water, otherwise the players will be drenched.
It is a very wet game. Play it outside, or use lots of towels and newspapers to soak up the splashes and to mop up people.

Bob Apple
Apples are hung in a doorway and each player must try to eat an apple while it swings. It must never be touched by hands, or *out* goes that person.
In Scotland an oat-cake called a bannock is smeared with treacle and used instead of an apple. Very messy!

Apple Love
At midnight apples are peeled, keeping the skin in a long spiralling piece which is then flung over the *left* shoulder. If the skin falls into a letter shape that will be the initial of the player's future love. Now eat the apple. It's far harder to peel the skin without a break.

Apple Blow
Rest a measuring stick, or something rigid such as a dowel between two chairs which should be placed about 60 cm apart.
Dangle two apples on strings from the stick so that they are about 2 cm apart.
Now, without touching an apple can you make them move towards the centre to bump each other?
Try blowing *between* the apples. Keep it up! Keep it up!

As well as games, tricks, riddles and rhymes, songs and spooky stories are shared at Hallowe'en. Sit close in a circle. Turn off the lights and begin . . .

THE HAIRY TOE

Once there was a Woman, went out to pick beans, and she found a Hairy Toe. She took the Hairy Toe home with her, and that night, when she went to bed, the wind began to moan and groan. Away in the distance she seemed to hear a voice crying,

"Where's my Hair-r-ry To-o-oe?
Who's got my Hair-r-ry To-o-oe?"

The Woman scrooched down, way down under the covers, and about that time the wind appeared to hit the house, *smoosh*, and the old house creaked and cracked like something trying to get in. The voice had come nearer, almost to the door now, and it said,

"Where's my Hair-r-ry To-o-oe?
Who's got my Hair-r-ry To-o-oe?"

She scrooched further down under the covers and pulled them tight around her head. The wind growled around the house like some big animal and r-rumbled over the chimney. All at once she heard the door cr-r-r-rack and *something* slipped in and began to creep over the floor.

The floor went cre-e-ak, cre-e-ak, at every step that Thing took towards her bed. The Woman could almost feel it bending over her head. Then in an awful voice it said:

"Where's my Hair-r-ry To-o-oe?
Who's got my Hair-r-ry To-o-oe?
YOU'VE GOT IT!"

The Hairy Toe is a good campfire story, or anytime story, as well as a favourite trick for Hallowe'en. Tell it your way but it's best told in the dark. At the end shout, "You've got it!" and grab the closest listener. Everyone, young and old, shares in the delicious spine-tingle no matter how many times the story has been heard before. It was first told in America and nobody remembers who invented it.

THE TREATS

Treats and food for Hallowe'en feasts were mostly made from harvest foods — nuts, apples, potatoes and pumpkins were favourites.

You can make these recipes yourself or with a grown-up to help. You can eat them all the year round, and do leave a clean kitchen, like the best cooks do.

Katie Crackernut's Devilled Almonds
Shell some nuts. They don't have to be almonds. Sometimes mixed nuts are favoured. Sprinkle the nuts on a well-greased scone tray. Dab with a little vegetable oil. Shake some pepper and salt and a little ground ginger over them. Bake ½ hour at 200°C(400°F) until the nuts are toasted. Cool and eat.

Jack o' lantern Pumpkin Seeds
Clean and wash the pumpkin seeds from the Jack o' lantern. Steam them in a double boiler to soften. This takes about 20 minutes. If you haven't a boiler put a cup in the bottom of a large saucepan. On top of the cup put a small metal bowl, or saucepan, or heat resistant container. Put the seeds into this and some *cold* water in the bottom of the big saucepan. Bring the water to boiling then turn down the heat to let the water gently simmer.

When the tough skins of the pumpkin seeds have softened, leave them to cool, then pat dry with a clean cloth or paper towel. Bake them in the oven in the same way as the Devilled Almonds.

72

Potatoes in Jackets

Scrub as many potatoes as you think you'll need. At least one for each potato-eater. Dry them, then wrap in foil. Place the potatoes on a scone tray and bake at 190°C(375°F) until tender. It will take about ¾ hour. Remove from the oven. Carefully unfold the foil and slit the top of each potato. Fill the slits with pieces of cheese and return the potatoes to the oven to cook a little longer. The cheese will melt. Yummy! This is how potatoes are sometimes eaten in Sweden. If you don't like cheese then fill the slits with butter and parsley, or a spoonful of sour cream sprinkled with chopped chives. Also yummy!

Baba Yaga Ice-blocks

You need a new pair of very clean kitchen gloves — the rubbery kind. Make up an ice-block mixture from fruit juice and water. Find someone to help fill the gloves with the mixture. Tie off the cuff very tightly. Prop the gloves in the freezer. When the ice-blocks have set, peel off the gloves and share out.

Baked Apples

You need one apple for each person. Cut out the core. Fill the hollow with a date or raisins, a sprinkle of brown sugar, a dusting of cinnamon, a squeeze of lemon juice, a few nuts or coconut sprinklings.

Put the apples into an oven-proof dish, cover the bottom with water, then bake at 180°C(350°F) until the apples are tender. Eat warm with cream, or ice-cream.

Carrot Cake
You will need:

   1½ cups of grated carrots: about 2 carrots
   ½ cup of chopped nuts. Walnuts are yummy
   2 eggs
   1 cup brown sugar
   1 cup of wholemeal flour
   ½ cup of self raising flour
   salt, just a pinch
   ¼ teaspoon each of nutmeg, cinnamon and ginger
   1 teaspoon of grated orange peel (Optional)
   ½ teaspoon bi-carb. soda
   ½ cup of melted margarine or oil
   1 large bowl
   wooden spoon
   well-greased ring tin, or your favourite tin

Put all the ingredients into the bowl and mix very well with the wooden spoon. Pour the mixture into the cake tin and bake at 180°C(350°F) for about 45 minutes, or until the testing straw comes out clean when prodded into the cake. Take from oven.

Leave the cake in the tin to cool a little, then turn it out carefully. Ice when cold. Orange or lemon icing tastes good. Decorate the cake with nuts, or be imaginative and find a spooky way to turn the cake into something special.

KATIE CRACKERNUTS

Once there was a King who had a daughter named Anne, whose beauty was so great no one noticed her step-sister. Neither girl cared one smidgeon about that, and they loved each other as many real sisters do.

However, Anne's loveliness vexed the Queen — an embittered jealous woman. It tormented her beyond reason. "Why should Anne be so beautiful and my Katie as plain as wheat-cake?" she repeatedly nagged at herself. In the end, she sought advice from the Henwife, a grisly old witch-woman if ever there was one. Together they plotted against Anne.

Next morning, and early it was, the Queen said, "Anne, my dear, go to the Henwife in the glen. Ask her for some breakfast eggs."

Anne set off as she'd been bid, taking a crust of bread from a shelf in the pantry to eat as she walked. "Do you have some eggs for my step-mother, the Queen?" she asked the Henwife.

"Aye, I do. Lift the lid from the pot, Princess, and look in," answered the Henwife.

Anne took up the lid and was doused in a swirling fog of fetid steam. She saw nothing in the pot, no eggs at all.

"Ach, go home to your mither," grumbled the Henwife. "Tell her to keep the pantry door locked."

When Anne delivered the impudent message the Queen looked annoyed but she made no comment about the Henwife's rudeness. Instead, next morning, and early it was, she sent Anne for eggs again. She herself shepherded the girl from the castle, checking first that the pantry door was locked.

So, an unfed hungry princess hurried along the road to the Henwife, until she saw some country folk picking peas in a field. Anne stopped to bid them good-day and while they chatted she nibbled a handful of tender green peas, then carried off a pocketful to eat as she walked.

"Lift the lid from the pot, Princess," said the Henwife as soon as the girl arrived. And for a second time Anne lifted the lid to an escaping cloud of stinking steam. There were not any eggs. The Henwife shrieked, babbling wild words which lost their sense in high-pitched screams. Anne drew back, turning to walk away and the Henwife calmed enough to yell, "Be off with you! Tell your mither a pot won't boil if the fire's away."

When Anne repeated the addle-pated, extraordinary message to the Queen she looked very grave and said, "We'll both go to the Henwife tomorrow, my dear."

And on the third morning, and early it was, the Queen stood beside Anne when she lifted the lid from the pot and a

sheep's head flew from it — Mercy! It fastened itself over Anne's bonny head.

Poor Anne! Poor Princess!

The Queen was over-joyed. The Henwife, wicked witch, crowed with glee. Her spell was successful.

But Katie was shocked and grieved to find her sister wandering about, heart-sick and weeping. She took a fine linen towel and wrapped it about Anne's head. "We can no longer live amongst such treachery," she told Anne. "We'll travel the world together and share our fortunes."

Katie led Anne from the castle and they travelled long roads to reach another kingdom. Katie found a refuge for Anne in an attic and work for herself in the castle's kitchen. "It's a strange household," Katie soon told Anne. "The King has two sons and one is sick enough to die. He will not wake, and no one knows what's ailing him. It is even more curious that whosoever sits to watch over the Prince each evening is never seen again."

No one now would watch over the Prince, although the King offered a peck of silver for the service. Then Katie offered, suspecting the Prince to be spell-bound.

Quietly she sat by his bedside. The clock struck twelve. The Prince who had been lying white and frail and still, silently rose and drew on his robes. Then, like a stick-thin shadow, he slipped from the room, treading softly down the stairs and out of the castle. It was as if he had been drawn away by an unseen power.

Katie followed the dazed Prince to the stables where he saddled his mare. No sooner was he in the saddle than Katie leapt up behind, feather-light. She rode with him to the Green Wood.

Trees were laden with nuts and as they passed under them Katie plucked handfuls from the branches, dropping them into her apron pockets.

Then, they rode from the Green Wood to a fern-green hill where the Prince drew bridle to call out dreamily, "Open! Open wide and let the Prince pass".

"And his Lady behind him!" Katie added swiftly.

A door, green with turf and moss and ferns, swung open. They passed through it to a magnificent hall, glowing with lights and bustling with chattering, laughing, noisy fairy folk. "The Prince! The Prince!" their magpie voices shouted and they buzzed about him, dragging at his clothes, pulling his arms, demanding that he should dance with each one. Dance

78

he did. He danced and danced until he fell exhausted to the floor. Fairies fanned his face, rubbed his cold hands and pushed him to his feet to dance again. He danced until he fell once more, exhausted. Again and again they revived the Prince and he danced until cock's crow.

Hastily, he mounted his mare. Katie sprang up behind him and they rode to the castle, through the Green Wood. Not once had the fairies suspected her presence in their hall.

Later, when the King anxiously visited his son's room he was relieved to see Katie sitting by the fire, cracking nuts. "My son looks a little better," he told her. "Would you stay with His Highness yet another night?" he asked. "I will reward you with gold."

"Very well," answered Katie, and so she spent the second night watching the Prince. Again, on the stroke of midnight, he rose from his bed as if spell-bound.

Again, Katie rode with him to the enchanted hall. Once more she entered with the Prince and the fairies neither sensed nor saw her and she wandered amongst them freely. In a corner, a tiny fairy child played with a glittery silvered wand, flashing it in swirls. Rustling and swinging, a fairy danced by, calling out cheerfully, "Be careful, Pillywiggins, of my bauble now! Three strokes from it and Katie's Anne will be as bonny as ever she was!"

Katie's heart swung right over with joy and she bowled a nut across the floor towards the child. She bowled another nut. Then another! Fascinated, little Pillywiggins watched them coming. His hand stretched out. He dropped the wand to grab a nut. Katie grabbed it and hid it under her apron. There it stayed until she rode with the Prince to the castle.

And how she ran, scrambling up the stairs to the attic and her sleeping sister. One-two-three times she touched the sheep's head. With the last stroke it fell from Anne's shoulders. Anne woke to find her own bonny head.

The sisters' joy and thankfulness was marvellous and then and there, they prepared to leave the castle, but first, Katie checked that her Prince was resting comfortably in his bed. And so the King found her and begged her to keep watch yet a third night. "Your son is more precious than gold or silver," she told the King. "I will stay for love of the Prince."

The third night was the same as the previous evenings, except that while the Prince danced Katie found Pillywiggins playing with a wee bird. "Just look at that!" scoffed a passing fairy with a flutter of glittering skirts. "Nobody knows that

80

just three mouthfuls of that birdie would break the spell binding our Prince. Just three mouthfuls and he'd be well again."

Uh-ah! So the Prince could be released from the enchantment. Katie rolled a handful of nuts towards the child. Bumping, clinking, they fanned out about his feet. His eyes shone and he clasped the bird to his chest, kicking the nuts with his feet . . . kicking, kicking. Katie waited for the kicking to stop and the rolling to stop, then she bowled her roundest nut. It bumped Pillywiggins's foot and bounced backwards. He grabbed it, dropping the bird. Kate whisked the bird up, under her apron.

At cock's crow, the Prince and Katie rode back to the castle where she plucked the bird and prepared it for the pot. Soon its savoury smell filled the Prince's room.

He stirred. He became restless, tossing about in his bed. His eyes moved under their lids, half-opened, closed again, then opened slowly, lazily. He sniffed and drowsily murmured, "I wish I could have a bite of whatever is stewing".

"And you shall," promised Katie.

He took a spoonful eagerly and enough strength flowed through him to enable him to prop himself up on his elbow and say, "If only I could have another mouthful!"

"You shall," answered Katie, spooning broth and flesh into his mouth.

"May I have another?" he asked, wide-awake and alert.

"You can have the potful!"

"Then I shan't eat it in bed," said the Prince, no longer ill and exhausted. His once-glazed eyes sparkled. His once-pale face now glowed with well-being. The spell was broken.

When the King visited his son he found him sitting by the

fire with Katie. Their heads were close together. They were laughing. They were cracking the last of Katie's nuts and sharing the kernels.

Of course, it wasn't long before the Prince believed that Katie was the most beautiful of Princesses. No one ever convinced him otherwise because that is the way of love. They were married, and it is said that Anne married his brother. And so the sisters shared their fortunes and . . .

"They lived happy and died happy
And never drank from a dry cappie."

OH, MRS WHITE!

Mrs White had a fright
In the middle of the night,
She saw a ghost eating toast
Halfway up a lamp post.

IN A DARK, DARK WOOD

In a dark, dark wood there was a dark, dark house;
And in the dark, dark house there was a dark, dark room;
And in the dark, dark room there was a dark, dark
  cupboard;
And in the dark, dark cupboard there was a dark, dark
  shelf;
And on the dark, dark shelf there was a dark, dark box;
And in the dark, dark box there was a . . . *ghost!*

Tell this story with lots of drama. It needn't be a ghost in
the box. What about a mouse? An elephant? Nothing at
all? Or a skeleton?

Make a skeleton from pipe-cleaners. Keep it hidden
while telling the story. At the end, whip it out suddenly to
dangle spookily in front of the listeners.

BELLINGTON SKELETON

To make Bellington you will need:
  7 white pipe-cleaners
  some black hat-elastic
Shape Bellington's skull with one cleaner.
Fasten two cleaners below his chin.
Twist and loop these to make his spine.
Use two cleaners to make bony arms.
Use two cleaners to make knobbled legs.
Tie the elastic to the top of Bellington's skull.
And that's it! He's finished.

84

GHOST OF JOHN

Have you seen the ___ ghost of John?

Long white bones and the rest all gone, ___

Ooh, ___ ooh, ___

Would-n't it be chil-ly with no skin on?

BIG BLACK BUCCA DHU

Once, and it certainly was once upon a time, an old Granny was off and away to play cards whenever she knew there was a game to be played somewhere. Rain or snow, sunshine day or cold dark night, the old dame was somewhere enjoying herself.

Oh, her family complained! They tsked. They tutted. They bleated to one another. "She'll fall in the dark night and break a leg!" "A woman of her age should be thankful to sit and knit!" "It's a scandal! Grans shouldn't gamble!" "The neighbours all gossip. Her habits are bad."

Complaining brought no reform to Gran's ways. No amount of persuading, reasoning, threatening, begging or scolding changed her. Let them cluck! The giddy old girl sallied out to yet another good time.

Then, surprisingly the heckling stopped. To tell the truth, the family had hatched a plan to frighten Gran into being a stay-at-home. They jingled some silver coins and convinced a serving-man that they would be his if he dressed in a white sheet and waylaid their Gran with ghostly wails and moans. After that, she'd be glad to mend her ways.

So, on Hallowe'en night, he put on the sheet. He took himself to wait on the darkest, loneliest patch of the homeward road. He waited two hours, then he waited three. The clouded sky cleared and a pale moon shone a thin light to stitch tree-shadow patches on the worn road. And along came the Dame, humming a song and watching where she put her feet.

"Aaa*aaaa*ah!" he rose up before her. "Aaa*aaaa*ah!" The sheet flapped, then slowly swam towards her. A drifting white shapeless thing!

Gran's hands fluttered. Her lips moved as if in a silent

prayer. Then, through the murk she peered and chirruped, "Hello, Ghostie! You are a gawky one!" Across the road she skipped, hitched herself up on the fence and leaned towards the ghost. "How are you this brave cold Hallowe'en?" she wanted to know. "Are you well inside your empty self?"

"Aaaaaaaah! Oooooooooh!" groaned the ghost.

"I'm sorry to hear that. You *are* ailing!" sympathised the Dame. "You're telling me then, that you're only out a-haunting because it's Hallowe'en, and folk expect it of you?" She nodded. "I know, I know! You'd rather be undisturbed and back in your old hidey-hole."

"Eeeeeeeeee!" shrieked the ghost, billowing itself before her. What a ghastly, unlovely, clumsy spirit!

Granny should have been shocked into ashen speechlessness. Not her! She edged closer. "Ahhh! You're a bright, brave little Ghostie!" Then she whispered. "You're going to need all your strength now. Don't look back, but the Big Black Bucca Dhu, the devil himself, is bearing down on you!"

The ghost croaked. A desperate little half-strangled cry. And he bolted. The sheet sailed out behind him like Monday's wash and she scampered behind him, clapping her hands and cheering, "Good boy, Bucca Dhu! Catch the little white Ghostie! Take him away with you!"

Scared almost senseless, the ghost, who was the serving man, you'll remember, shilly-shallied off course, tripped over the sheet and tumbled into a ditch where he quaked until sunrise, too terrorized to scramble out. It was a long time before he was right in the head again. Still, he did escape Granny's devil friend, if such a horror ever existed.

And after that, the Dame was left to live her life out as she wished, which was the way it should have been in the first place.

GHOST MOBILES

You will need:
    137cm square of an old sheet
    wire coathanger
    newspaper
    string
    a felt pen or paint

Pad the hook of the coathanger with newspaper until it is a skull shape.
Tie it firmly into place.
Put the sheet over the padded hook, making sure that the sheet hangs evenly.
Secure the sheet to the hook with some string under the ghost's chin.
Draw on a ghostly face.
Sew a string to the top of the skull and hang up the ghost where a draught will move the sheet. *Oooowah!*

To make a smaller mobile you will need:
    paper tissues
    cotton-wool balls
    coathanger
    thread
    a felt pen or luminous paint

Make a little ghost by placing a cotton-wool ball in the centre of a paper tissue. This is the head. Tie it firmly with thread. Draw on facial features.
Sew a thread to the top of the head. Attach its free end to the bottom of the coathanger.
Make as many more ghosts as you like. Hang them at different lengths for the best effect.
Decide where to hang your mobile.

89

Australia's best known ghost is of a swagman who stole a sheep and came to a watery end in a billabong.

WALTZING MATILDA
(Carrying a Swag)

Oh! there once was a swag-man camped by a bill-a-bong,—

Un-der the shade of a Cool-a-bah tree; And he

sang as he looked at his old bil-ly boil-ing,—

"Who'll come a-waltz-ing Ma-til-da with me?"

Who'll come a-waltz-ing Ma-til-da, my darl-ing,—

Who'll come a-waltz-ing Ma-til-da with me?

Waltz-ing Ma-til-da and lead-ing a wat-er bag—

Who'll come a-waltz-ing Ma-til-da with me.

Down came a jumbuck to drink at the water-hole,
  Up jumped the swagman and grabbed him in glee;
And he sang as he stowed him away in his tucker-bag,
  "You'll come a-waltzing Matilda with me."

Down came the Squatter a-riding his thoroughbred;
  Down came Policemen — one, two and three.
"Whose is the jumbuck you've got in your tucker-bag?
  You'll come a-waltzing Matilda with me."

But the swagman, he up and he jumped in the water-hole,
  Drowning himself by the Coolabah tree;
And his ghost may be heard as it sings in the Billabong
  "Who'll come a-waltzing Matilda with me?"

A. B. (Banjo) Paterson

QUEEN NEFERTITI

Spin a coin, spin a coin,
All fall down:
Queen Nefertiti
Stalks through town.

Over the pavements
Her feet go clack,
Her legs are as tall
As a chimney stack.

Her fingers flicker
Like snakes in the air,
The walls split open
At her green-eyed stare;

Her voice is thin
As a ghost of bees;
She will crumble your bones,
She will make you freeze.

Spin a coin, spin a coin,
All fall down.
Queen Nefertiti
Stalks through town.

Nefertiti is a bit of a horror. Invent some strange music
suitable for such a queen. Use empty tins, spoons, stones
shaken in a tin, flapping paper, anything that makes a sound.
Experiment. The sounds could be taped. You could move like
Nefertiti. She's really horrible! What would her face be like?
Create a face for her from play make-up. What were her
clothes? Invent some for a very strange queen.

SPOOKY COIN

Here's something else to try:
Sprinkle some water on the top of a milk
bottle, or a large soft-drink bottle. Sprinkle
water on a coin. Put the coin on top of the
bottle. Grasp the bottle with both hands.
Spread out your fingers, just below the bottle's
neck. Count slowly to 30. Has the coin
moved? Count until it lifts upwards.

Wow! Are ghostly fingers trying to steal it?

No. The warmth of your hands has
expanded the cold air in the bottle.

RIDDLE THRILLS

How can you enter a haunted house?
With a skeleton key.

How can you fatten a ghost?
With goulash and spooketti.

What is a spook's favourite ride?
A roller ghoster.

Can a witch tell the time?
Yes, with a witch watch.

What is bigger than a monster and lighter than
a bird?
A monster's shadow.

What would you have if you crossed a ghost
and a black bird?
A scare-crow.

THE SPUNKY

The Spunky he went like a sad little flame,
   All, all alone.
All out on the zogs and a-down the lane,
   All, all alone.
A tinker came by that was full of ale,
And into the mud he went head-over-tail,
   All, all alone.

A crochety farmer came riding by,
   All, all alone.
He cursed him low and he cursed him high,
   All, all alone.
The Spunky he up and led him astray,
The pony were floundered until it were day,
   All, all alone.

There came an old Granny — she see the small ghost,
    All, all alone.
"Yew poor liddle soul all a-cold, all a-lost,
    All, all alone.
I've give 'ee a criss-cross to save 'ee hide,
Be off to the church and make merry inside."
    All, all alone.

The Spunky he laughed, "Here, I'll galley no more!"
    All, all alone.
And off he did wiver and in at the door,
    All, all alone.
The souls they did sing for to end his pain,
There's no little Spunky a-down the lane,
    All, all alone.

The *Spunky* is a Will o' the Wisp, once thought by some people to be the wandering spirit of a baby who had died before being baptised.

The *tinker* wandered about the countryside mending pots and pans.

The *zogs* is a marshy place where Will o' the Wisps might be seen at night.

Criss-cross is to christen, or to name with the sign of the cross.

Galley is to frighten.

Wiver is a wandering-floating-quivering movement and just the word to describe the Will o' the Wisp or a Spunky.

96

THE DEAD MOON

Once, when strange things happened, Boggles with leather noses, and skinny-limbed Hobgoblins, and those old Gangling Waifs and other half-dead Things crept and crawled from the bog on the dark nights when the moon didn't shine. They joined with other nasties to harm both man and beast with their evil doings. It was their delight to trip travellers into the oozing slime, or pull them into the sludge with snake-thin vines. And they snatched and scratched and prodded from bushes, tormenting and maddening poor wretches until they fell to their knees exhausted. Then the Will o' the Wisps teased, dancing ahead with fitful lanterns tied to their backs, until ways were lost and the victims sucked into dark mud-holes.

In time the Moon heard of the wickedness in the bog. To put an end to the horrors she herself went there at the month's end. She stepped down to the watery places, walking softly and showing no light; her body wrapped in her darkest cloak and her glister-bright hair covered by a hood, the deepest colour of the night's sky. Only her bare feet glowed gently, showing a pale shimmering light which glossed the quaking mud with silver streaks, and sometimes glanced across spiked grass tussocks, or briefly spangled the bare spiked branches of straggling bushes.

97

All at once, the stillness of the sluggish, dank, shadow-thick bog erupted into hair-raising, nightmarish noise and movement. Witches shrieked and their cats howled. Owls hooted. Boggles and Nasties screamed an argument. Will o' the Wisps frisked from their hiding holes, swirling their deceitful lanterns. Hobgoblins pranced and fought Horn-kneed Imps. A weirdly-awful Thing flashed green swivelling eyes from the murky water and strange lustre shapes stretched white arms like branches from the slime.

Unafraid and silent, Lady Moon glided from path to stone, looking upon them all and listening to their spine-chilling voices. Then, her foot slipped, missing a stone. She grasped a willow branch to regain her balance. It snaked about her wrist, tightening like a wire rope, imprisoning her.

She struggled wordlessly, trying to free her hand until — through the blanket-thick darkness — a lad stumbled towards her, clawed by cackling Boggles, jostled by Goblins, slapped off the path by screeching Witches who urged their cats to leap upon his back. A Will o' the Wisp with a whirling lantern, half-blinded the lad, then waltzed ahead, enticing him off the path into the bog.

"Stay! Wait!" cried out Lady Moon, throwing back her head. The hood slipped. Light streamed from the pale gold of her hair. In its radiance the lad saw his danger, the bog-holes at his feet. In tinsel-bright moonlight he found his homeward path and ran for dear life.

The Bog Horrors let him go, rushing upon a better prey,

half-strangling Lady Moon to dowse her shimmering light. They cursed her. They beat her. They pushed her downwards into the stinking rubbish of decayed leaves and slime. The Moon! The Moon! The Lady Moon! She was theirs! A prisoner! She'd *never* shine again!

They raved with excitement, the joy of an unexpected victory. They pranced and hopped and skipped, then a Hairy One demanded to know the best way to be rid of the Moon forever. They argued and squabbled, quarrelled and shouted, spat, scratched, kicked and hurt in spiteful disagreement. By dawn there was no agreement. So late! So late! They must slink into bog-holes and dark, sunless crannies. Perhaps they would kill the Moon, come the next black curtain of night. And so they trampled her cruelly into the slime and rolled a great stone over her, sinking her deeply into a watery grave. She could stay there for a night or a year. Who cared? There was no escape for Lady Moon.

And there followed night after night after night when forlorn white stars pricked through the darkness. Night after night when the sky was a misery of blackness. Night after night when no moon shone. People waited and longed for her return but she never rose above the Bogland. And each night the Evil Ones' howls and screeches moved closer to the village, and no one dared venture out at night, although night lamps burned in windows to guide wanderers home. Fearful that the Nasties would invade their houses, the villagers consulted their Wise-Woman-on-the-hill.

She went to her learned books, she looked into a crystal ball, stared at her reflection in a crooked mirror and stirred a stew-pot bubbling with herbs, both sour and sweet. She could tell them nothing of Lady Moon. The Moon was lost.

Then, the boy who had been saved from the Bog Horrors

by her beams, recalled with awe, "Lady Moon has not shone since that night! They must have her in the bog! The Evil Ones have stolen the Moon!"

Again the Wise-Woman-on-the-hill consulted her books, the crystal ball, the crooked mirror and the brewing herbs. There was a way to save the Moon. "The strongest and bravest must arm themselves each with a hazel twig, close their lips over a pebble and never speak whilst within the water places," she warned. "Lady Moon will be lost forever if the three trials are not born."

Both men and women, all strong and brave, marched to the bog. Each carried a hazel twig. Teeth clenched smooth round river pebbles. No one spoke.

About them the air thickened with sighs, whispers and hisses. Slimy hands stretched forth from slush, bony fingers clutched at jackets, puff-balls of light darted at their eyes, twigs slapped faces, winged things brushed their cheeks, shrieks and screams filled them with fear, yet no one spoke, no one paused. And they found the place where the huge stone buried the Moon.

And they pulled it from the squelching, slippery mud and gazed upon the beautiful glowing face of Lady Moon who smiled at them. Her beams dazzled their eyes and they drew back as she rose from the mud. And their ears were filled with the dying moans of the thwarted Boggles and Hobgoblins, the Nasties and other Evil Ones, who disappeared . . . tottering, slinking, crawling into bog-holes and slimy hidden corners.

Above the murky waters, above the snags, above the ragged bushes and stunted trees, rose Lady Moon. She drifted skywards in slow majesty. Her clear white radiance lit the Boglands, showing the villagers the safe paths to home, the lonely paths known to this very day.

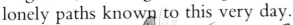

IS THE MOON TIRED?

Is the Moon tired? She looks so pale
Within her misty veil;
She scales the sky from east to west,
And takes no rest.

Before the coming of the night
The Moon shows papery white;
Before the dawning of the day,
She fades away.

Christina Rossetti

INGRID'S CHANGELING

Once, a lazy old Dwarf, wanting to be petted and waited-upon, threw a baby from its cradle and jumped in himself. Luckily, waiting Fairy-folk caught the child and were delighted to steal him, this fair-haired bonny little boy.

Ingrid, his nurse-maid, knew straight away that her charge had been swapped for a changeling, yet his doting parents behaved as if it were their own wee son still in the cradle. Love for their child seemed to have blinded them, strange as it may seem. The Changeling was as ugly as a warty toad, scrawny as an old parsnip and big-footed like a monkey. "*Wah! Wah! Wah!*" Its squalling voice almost drove Ingrid mad. Day and night, up and down the stairs she sprinted, attending to its

wants. It bawled for food. Great bowls of it were gobbled up and then it screamed for more and more.

Before long Ingrid had to peel fifty potatoes and chop six cabbages and fry twenty rashers of bacon for the Changeling's supper alone. Every scrap of the wholesome food was swallowed but the Greedy One didn't grow taller or fatter. Oh yes, Ingrid knew it was a Changeling in the cradle, not the family's sweet little son. "How can I convince Master and Mistress?" she asked herself in torment.

That evening, after she had settled the child and his parents had left the nursery, Ingrid tip-toed back along the hall to peek through the slit in the nursery door. The Changeling dozed contentedly in the cradle. Then, from the distance came the click of a closing door and she knew that her Master and Mistress were about to eat their supper. Obviously the Changeling knew this too. Its eyes flew open. It sprang from the cradle. Up the wall it scrambled like a cat! Over the rafters! Like a monkey it swung by one arm, kicking at the air. Then down to the floor! Plop! Round the room! Round the room! It ran on all fours, chuckling and cackling. Then up on the table! It pitched the freshly ironed laundry to the floor, over its head and at the walls in a snow-storm of baby clothes and linen. Combs, brushes, soap, powder, toys and pins followed, bowled across the room to hit some unseen target. Then, the Changeling pummelled a pillow. Teeth tore its embroidered covering, skinny hands punched until feathers oozed out, floating, falling, nose-tickling feathers.

A-a-achoo! Ingrid sneezed as she rushed into the room. Her eyes blinked closed for an instant only, long enough for the Changeling to bounce back into the cradle. It pulled at the coverings, shut its dark eyes tightly, squashed its face small and screamed, "*Wah! Wah! Wah!*"

104

Ingrid let it bellow. She closed the door to keep in the noise and tidied the room. "Brat! Troll-child!" she muttered. "That little wretch yells like a wild thing and eats enough for ten grown men!" she complained to the servants when at last she went wearily to the kitchen. "I'm run off my feet fetching it jugs of milk, bowls of broth and tureens of buttered potatoes."

"Just bring your bread and cheese to . . ." began Cook, never finishing her invitation.

Startled cries from the littlest Chambermaid alarmed them all. She pointed a shaking finger to the cellar door. "S-something is d-down there that-that-that shouldn't be there!" she quavered.

A light of astounding brightness dazzled under the door.

"Pull yourself together, girl!" scolded Cook. "Someone has left a lamp burning, that's all." She looked accusingly at the Groom.

"*No one* has been to the cellar," he flashed back. "We're all here. There was no light there moments ago. Who lit it?"

It was a marvellous, over-bright light, a starkly white and steady light which magnified crumbs and sweepings, scratches and blackened pock-marks, dirt-crammed cracks and chips on the worn red tiles as far as the faded hearth rug.

"It must be Master or Mistress," decided Cook.

"How could it be? We've not seen them pass. They must go through the kitchen to reach the cellar," argued the Groom.

"I'm frightened!" whispered the littlest Chambermaid.

"I'm not," declared Ingrid. "I'll go down and see."

"Don't! Stay here! That light isn't natural!" warned the Groom, not offering to go himself. "We'll all stay here."

"I'm not scared. I'm not scared of anything after that awful child upstairs. There can't be anything worse in the cellar," Ingrid told them and opened the cellar door.

The light was blinding. She shielded her eyes against its brilliance, pausing briefly before she stepped down one . . . two . . . three steps. She halted, looked about the cellar, her eyes searching between the casks, over the shelves, into corners, about the floor and even the ceiling. The cellar was empty and very silent. There seemed to be no source for the light. It shone from everywhere, yet nowhere. Puzzled, she swung her eyes about the cellar once more.

"Huh! Since you're peeping, then I'm throwing!" rasped a voice.

"If you're throwing, then I'm catching!" challenged Ingrid.

Zzzzpt! A bundle sailed across the cellar. She stretched out and caught it. Nothing but a bundle of soft rags! Just rags! Then it whimpered. "You're our own Little One!" she whispered, recognizing the cry. She pulled away the rags. The child was unharmed. It was as plump and as rosy as ever, sweet-smelling and clean.

She ran with the boy from the cellar and slammed the door. There was a scuttle of little feet, or was there? The light snapped off, but Ingrid, heading everyone from the kitchen, cluttered up the stairs.

The cradle was empty. The cantankerous, quarrelsome greedy Changeling was gone. Ingrid re-made the little bed, lovingly settled her dear baby in it and softly crooned a lullaby while she rocked the cradle.

The lazy old Dwarf and his cellar friends were never seen again, and thank goodness for that.

BABY IN A CRADLE

You may need a little help from someone to knit the baby's clothes, but do as much as you can yourself.

First, collect together some scraps of pale coloured wool, 4 ply is best. One pair of 3¼ mm (no. 10) knitting needles. One small wooden bead. Needle and thread. A felt pen. A scrap of material in your favourite colour. An empty match box. Glue.

To Make the Baby's Clothes
Cast on 16 stitches
Knit 1 row in plain knitting 1 row in purl

This is called stocking stitch.
Continue in stocking stitch for another 8 rows.
End with a purl row.
Knit two stitches together to the end of the row.

You should have 8 stitches left on the needle.

To Make The Hood
On the 8 stitches knit 6 rows of stocking stitch.
On the 7th row knit 4 stitches only.
Now knit one stitch from each end together.
This will make the top of the hood.
Cast off.
Your knitting should be the shape shown.
Sew the bottom and the sides of the sleeping bag together.
Sew the wooden bead into the hood to make the baby's head.
Mark eyes on the bead.
There is no need to stuff the knitted doll.
It would be too fat to fit the match box.

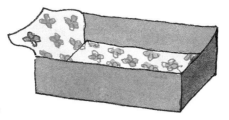

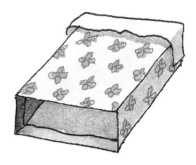

To Make The Bed
Line the match-box tray with the material.
Allow enough to fold over the top into a
little pillow.
Fold under the raw edges so that the
bed-clothes fit neatly and glue them to the
bottom of the tray.
Cut another strip of material just long enough
to fold round the match-box lid. It should be a
little longer than the lid so there is enough to
overlap like the top of a sheet.
Glue the material in place on the lid.
Leave the match box to dry.
Tuck the doll into the tray and fit on the lid.
Now you have a pocket-sized cradle and a
littling.

In the once-upon-a-time a changeling was never a welcomed
guest. Stolen human babies, especially fair-headed ones, were
replaced by a sickly elf, or an old gnome. The best way to
regain the proper baby was to trick the changeling into
revealing its age by pretending to brew beer in a goose's egg.
"I'm old, old, old but I've never seen such a thing!" the
changeling would whine and would be whisked away.
Immediately, the human babe would be returned.

Dwarfs, goblins and trolls were underground elves and
often skilled iron workers. The trolls, long-limbed creatures,
also were famous for their cattle and mostly lived in the high
lonely mountain places of Sweden, Norway and Denmark,
and absolutely hated humans or animals to invade their
territory.

KIDMUS

Kidmus the troll, had a poker-straight nose almost as long as your arm, and it was apple-red on the knobbled end. His eyes were red-rimmed too, and saucer large. Other trolls thought he was handsome enough; you certainly wouldn't have. Kidmus was such a crotchety, sour, bad-tempered creature! He enjoyed being alone, and indeed, he lived peacefully enough until . . . people built a house-of-sorts beside *his* mound.

There were two people — Man who hunted and fished for food, and Woman who spun and wove wool for their clothes. Their most precious possession was her spinning wheel with a golden knob, a solid gold knob. That was something to treasure, to be proud of and to boast about.

Well, imagine the to-do there was when the knob jolted off the wheel, clattered to the floor and rolled out of the door.

"Lawks-a-mercy!" spluttered Woman. She chased the precious knob but it couldn't be found on the path, or in the grass.

Her search was thorough, and she searched again and again until Man hove in sight, shouting, "What are you doing, poking about like an old hen?"

"I sat and I spun and while I spun our golden knob flew off the spinning wheel," she whimpered. "I can't find it."

"Kidmus will have it," said he and trotted to the grassy mound. *Thud! Whack!* He belted a stick on the side of the mound.

"Who knocks so loud on my house?" answered a muffled yell.

"It's your neighbour. Woman wants back the knob of gold from her spinning wheel."

"What will she take if I keep it?"

"A cow who gives four buckets of milk."

"A cow she shall have!"

At once, the side of the mound creaked open and a cow strolled out. That evening at milking time, she gave four buckets of milk, and more . . . enough to fill the laundry tub as well . . . and the stew-pan, then the kettle, the-pots-and-the -basins-the-teacups-the-mugs and whatever else would hold liquid. Trolls' cows are generous milkers and this one's gift of

milk was too much. Only when every vessel owned by Man and Woman was filled to over-flowing did she stop giving milk.

"What are we going to do with all this?" grizzled Woman.

"Make some porridge," Man told her.

"We haven't any oatmeal, and we haven't a spare pot."

"Then Kidmus can give us both."

And Man thudded his stick against the grassy mound. "Who knocks so loudly?" groaned Kidmus.

"It's your neighbour, dear Kidmus. Woman wants more payment for her knob of purest, most precious gold."

"What does she want this time?"

"Oatmeal and a pot to cook it in."

"Very well."

The side of the mound jerked open. A barrel of oatmeal bounced out. An iron pot hurtled out.

Soon the oatmeal bubbled and plopped in the iron pot which dangled over the fire.

Soon they ate piping hot porridge served with creamy milk. They ate. They ate. They ate. They could not empty the pot. Indeed, it still held as much porridge as when the first spoonful was ladled from it.

"We'll never reach the bottom of the pot, even if we eat for a month," complained Man. "What are we going to do with it?"

"Give it away."

"To whom? No one lives nearby."

"We could give it to Saint Peter."

"My good Woman, how could we reach him?"

"By ladder to heaven, silly Man. Go and tell Kidmus he owes yet another payment for the knob. Ask him for a ladder to reach heaven."

"Yes! I'll do that."

Man beat at the grassy mound, thrashing and bruising the grass. "Who knocks?" barked Kidmus, holding his aching head.

"It's your neighbour, dear Kidmus! Woman needs one last payment for her purest, most precious and rarest knob of gold."

"I've paid for that knob twice-over," snarled Kidmus.

"No, not quite enough."

"I have! I have! I have!"

"No, you have not! Our last request is small. Just a ladder to reach heaven, no more than that."

"*Take it!*"

The side of the mound blasted open. Out pitched a ladder.

Man propped it against the mound and began to climb. "Bring out the porridge pot, Woman!" he sang.

"It's heavy!" she panted as she lugged it from the house.

"Bring it up to me. I'll carry it first."

She struggled up behind him and handed over the pot. Then they climbed the ladder towards heaven. Up and Up! Up! Up! Taking turns to haul up the pot.

"It's a long way to heaven," cried out Woman.

"That's to be expected."

"It will also be a long way back to home."

"That's to be expected."

"Oh Man! The ladder is swaying!"

"That, too, is to be expected."

"I am feeling dizzy. Oh-oh! My head spins. Man! Take the pot!"

Man held a rung with one hand, stretched down the other and took the pot. As he straightened, Woman grabbed his ankles. "Let go! How can I climb when you hold me?" he grouched.

"My head! My head spins . . . and spins!" she wailed.

113

"Nonsense!" He pulled his foot from her grasp. The ladder swayed . . . swayed, swayed wide. She shrieked and toppled over and over to the ground. Down he came after her. Down came the pot, splattering porridge, *plummetty-thud*.

Breathless and battered and bruised they lay on the grass for minutes before they pulled themselves together and staggered into the house. "I'll never ask that troll for another thing," vowed Man.

And inside the mound, Kidmus shook with laughter until he doubled-up with mirth and his nose bumped the ground. Never again was he tormented by those two.

WHO'S THAT TAPPING?

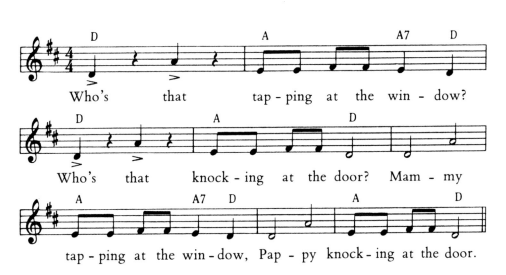

Who's that tap-ping at the win-dow?
Who's that knock-ing at the door? Mam-my
tap-ping at the win-dow, Pap-py knock-ing at the door.

LISUNKA'S LITTLE BLACK POT

Once, and long ago it was, a Leshy was Lord of the Forest. All the trees belonged to the Leshy, and the animals and birds. All the grass. All things green. If a herdsman grazed his cattle in the meadows then he paid for the grass with a gift of fresh milk for the Leshy. No one dared cross the Forest Lord. Never! Punishment followed quickly — a clout from the Leshy's Great Bear which was enough to flatten the strongest man.

The Leshy was a miserly horror. Should any misguided wanderer rest in a deserted forest hut overnight, the Leshy, violent with rage, pounded on the door. Then, howling, shrieking, sometimes moaning, he whirled like a wind-storm, as if to uproot the hut from the ground. The terrified traveller escaped at first light, and if he was fortunate, he also escaped seeing the Leshy, who was terrible just to glimpse.

He had feet like a goat's, clawed hands, grey skin. No eyebrows. No eyelashes. Just a fiery eye, a single mean little eye glaring and glowering from under his low bump of a brow, or staring through a tangle of green lank hair. The Leshy wore a greasy sheepskin hanging like a caftan over his body which changed its size at the Leshy's whim to forest-tree tall, or grass-blade short. Lisunka, his wife, was not a scrap better to look upon, and she was said to be just as ferocious.

The forest was safe only during the depths of winter when the Leshies curled under a blanket of snow, to sleep until spring. Beside them snored the Great Bear and in a way, each guarded the other. Most people stayed out of the forest, no matter what, even a sleeping Leshy was to be feared.

At one time Anna, searching for a certain moss which she needed for her dye pot, ventured into the trees. Alert and watchful for danger, she quickly peeled dark, plushy moss from rock and stones. Suddenly, she paused to listen. She was sure she had heard the cry of a baby, a long distressed wail which ended in silence as if the child held its breath. It came from deeper in the forest. "No babe would be there," she told herself. "It must be an animal or a bird."

The cry came again, and again. Piercing, anxious, heart-broken cries which ended in sobs. "It's not a child. It's a Leshy trick!" Anna decided, picking up her basket and running from the forest.

When she paused for breath she could still hear the sobs. They were faint and far-off, but went on and on. Lonely grieving whimpers which made Anna's heart ache. Only a frightened child would cry so long and piteously.

She left the basket and went back towards the weeping. Stumbling over tree roots, pushing through thorny under-growth and bushes she tracked the cries to a clearing, and she saw the child — small and hunched and shaking from cold and fear.

"Poor little mite!" murmured Anna. "Don't cry, Baby!" she called. The Child looked up, sorrow crumpling its face. Small arms stretched out to Anna. She scooped it up, wrapped it in her shawl, rocked it, soothed it with words and tried to quell her own panic and her urge to run away. She willed herself to comfort the child, forced herself to look at it.

From head to feet the baby was covered in green fur. Its skin was pale grey. It had closed its single eye to a slit in its forehead. Anna held a Leshy child! Its head trustingly rested on her shoulder. It clung to her, clutching as if it would never let go. It listened to her voice and its sobs lessened, until the troubled baby, warm and re-assured, drifted into sleep.

"Perhaps if I leave it between tree roots someone will find it," Anna thought but as she put the baby under a tree she changed her mind, taking it back into her arms. "A Leshy may not pass for a long time." She couldn't bear the infant to be frightened again, and perhaps cold and hungry. "I dare not take it home. What shall I do?" she worried.

There was no time to find a solution. Lisunka crashed through the undergrowth, shouting hysterically, "You, Woman! Have you seen the Little One?"

"Be at peace!" Anna called back. "He is safe." She held out the child. "Hush! He sleeps."

Lisunka snatched the child and stared at Anna so maliciously, so suspiciously that Anna stepped backwards. Lisunka followed, shouting into her face, "*You* stole my babe! I will kill you!"

"Stop shouting! You will wake him!" Anna hushed Lisunka. "And I didn't steal him," she hissed indignantly, her voice hardly a whisper. "He was crying in the clearing. I heard him and comforted him. You should take more care of your child." Anna prodded Lisunka with an accusing finger.

Lisunka stepped back now. She muttered sheepishly, "Aaaah! You worry for him! You worry that my growls will wake him. You worry that I neglect him. I do *not*!" Her voice rose in denial, then dropped to confide in a hoarse whisper, "You know how it is with small ones. He ran off. Toddled away when my back was turned. Gone as quickly as a fox shakes its tail. And you must go quickly, too. Come! We'll go to the path from the forest before the Forest Lord himself comes after you."

Lisunka shouldered her baby and hoofed off in long strides with Anna running at her heels, running to keep up, running to the edge of the forest.

Anna leant against a tree to regain her breath and Lisunka dumped the baby into her arms while she mumbled and foraged amongst some rocks. "Take this!" she rumbled, exchanging the baby for a little iron pot. Its sides were burned gloomy black and it smoked from orange-red coals which glowed in its depths. "It is my gift to you, little Mother," Lisunka told Anna.

Anna gravely accepted the gift, thanking Lisunka with a curtsy. At least the strange offering could be used as a small dye-pot, Anna thought as they parted. A very small dye-pot, indeed!

She put the pot on her hearth, then busied herself preparing the moss to colour her wool.

Much later, when Anna took the dyed yarn from the simmering pot, her foot knocked against Lisunka's gift and sent it rattling across the floor. "Bother!" Anna looked down, expecting to see a scattering of cinders on the floor. From the mouth of the pot a trail of gold nuggets winked and glinted in the firelight. Big nuggets and all gold! Anna had been well rewarded for her kindness to the Leshy's babe. Oh, yes!

HUSH, LITTLE BABY!

The bough rocks the bird now,
The flower rocks the bee,
The breeze rocks the lily,
The wind rocks the tree.

And I rock you, Baby,
So softly to sleep,
You must not awaken
Till daisy-buds peep.

TIE-DYEING

Anna used moss to dye newly spun wool. It would have turned a yellow-green. Spinach leaves, onion skins, nut shells, rose petals, blackberries and other things were once used to stain cloth.

You can try your hand at dyeing without Anna's hard work by experimenting with cold-water dyes from the chemist, or other shops.

You'll need:
    a piece of old sheeting or some plain coloured material
    cold-water dye of one or more colours
    string
    scissors
    a large pot

There could be a mess, so clean up afterwards, of course. Read the instructions which come with the dye.

Fold the material in concertina gathers, or into bunches.

Tie the bunches off at intervals with string. Or just tie knots.

Dip the material into the dye water — part of it, or all of it.

Take it out.

Rinse well.

Unfold the material and discover blotched patterns.

THE DRAGON

There's a drag - on crawl - ing round, crawl - ing round the
room. Do not get too close or it will
sure - ly spell your doom. A drag - on's al - ways
look - ing for some - thing to munch.
If you don't watch out, you may be his lunch.

WINGLESS DRAGON

To make a little dragon you will need:
  40cm of thin wire
  foil
  felt pen
  patience
Cut the wire in half.
Cut *one* half into half.
You now have 3 pieces.
Shape them into a skeleton
as the picture shows.
Make sure that the wire is firmly looped.
Build up the dragon's shape with strips of foil.
Coloured wrappings from chocolates and
sweets can be used too. A few lumps and
bumps look very dragonish. Use a large piece
of foil for the last layer and squeeze it on well.
Give the dragon black spot eyes. Can you
make him look more ferocious?

ROTHERHAM DRAGON

This dragon had two furious wings
Each upon each shoulder,
With a sting in his tail, as long as a flail
Which made him bolder and bolder.

He had long claws and in his jaws
Four and forty teeth of iron,
With hide as strong as any buff
Which did him round environ.

SAINT GEORGE AND THE DRAGON

Long ago when dragons still breathed fire across the lands, a huge and monstrous loathly worm of a beastie beset the fair city of Silene. The fiery, jaw-snapping, bone-crushing, old poison-puffer had completely devastated the countryside. He slashed his tail and slew every brave man who sallied out against him, until all who lived in Silene were in danger of being devoured.

For a short respite, the King and his men were able to satisfy the dragon's greed by feeding it sheep, until none remained. Then, to their shame, a law was passed, decreeing that two children, or young people were to be thrown to the dragon each day. The victims were chosen by lots. Thus, noble and peasant, rich and poor were treated equally.

The city grieved to lose their children. Then the name of the Princess Sabra was drawn.

"Take my gold. Take my crown but spare my only child," begged the King.

"We cannot. You passed the law and already many children have died," the King was told. "It is your turn to give up a child."

The King was beside himself with grief and despair. "I love my daughter. It is my wish that she should reign as your Queen," he wept.

But his pleas could not change the law. If he shielded the Princess, then she would be taken from him by force, and the palace burned. However, as the King of Silene had been a just ruler, the City of Silene allowed him eight days grace.

Alas, on the eighth day Princess Sabra received her father's blessing then walked calmly and courageously from the palace gates. As she raised her hand in farewell a wistful smile hid her fear, and the people mourned to see her pass — their Princess, a small figure gowned as splendidly as a royal bride.

They left her, chained to a rock lying close to the dragon's lake. Trembling, she waited, listening for the dragon's approach.

Soon, hoof-beats drummed over dry, hard ground and scales clinked, jangling in a harsh rhythm. She closed her eyes, not wanting to look, and prepared herself for the searing, blistering breath of the dragon against her skin. She waited. She waited. The hoof-beats halted. A voice called, "Fair Lady! Why do you stand weeping?"

Sabra's eyes opened to behold a Knight, bestride his great horse, a sword at his side and a spear in his hand.

"Ride for your life, or you too, will perish!"

"Ride for my life? What danger is here for me? I am George of Cappadocia, a Christian Knight."

"Sir George, I await the dragon whose meal I shall be."

"Then, by the Grace of God, I shall save you," vowed George.

He unshackled her chains and as he worked, the waters of the lake were disturbed, moving as if ruffled by the wind. Then rapidly the water surged upwards into arcs of foaming waves and the dragon lumbered from the lake's depths. Its jaws snapped. Its tail lashed. It snorted and belched fire.

George of Cappadocia raised his hand to shape the sign of the cross then mounted his horse, wheeled about and charged. His spear sliced through the air. Straight and true it pierced the dragon's throat, maddening the beast with pain. It floundered, then crawled from the water, coughing flames, turning its head, swivelling its eyes, searching for its attacker.

It reared. Bat wings unfolded. The dragon hung in the air with unleashed claws, ready to strike. It crashed downwards to crush the Knight who side-stepped his mount, just beyond reach of the opened mouth and cruel claws.

Then he flung himself from the saddle to rush at the crouching beast. The sword slashed. The dragon clawed and scrabbled, heckled by this tiresome ant of a man. The great tail heaved and thudded. Evil-smelling poisonous smoke fogged the battle and the bleary-eyed, wounded dragon knew not where to strike.

Unseen, the Knight drew closer. He plunged the sword through scales and flesh, plunged deep, deep into the dragon's breast. It sank to its knees, toppled sideways and collapsed hissing into soft dust.

"Lady, take off your girdle and bind it about the dragon's head," the Knight told Sabra.

The Princess tied the girdle to the beast's head and lo and behold it rose to its feet and followed her like a docile hound on a leash, to the city!

As they approached the people fled in terror. "Do not fear the dragon! Put your trust in the Lord!" George of Cappadocia called to them. "It was my trust which helped me to overcome fear and the dragon."

Then, before them all, he withdrew his sword and smote off the dragon's head.

The King and his subjects were awe-struck. "I will give you silver and gold for this deed," declared the King.

"Give it to the poor," answered the Knight. "Build a church in this place, where your dragon died." Then, blessing the City of Silene and its people he left them to ride to a crusade in the Holy Lands.

The Knight had many more adventures before his life ended in a martyr's death. Later crusaders built a chapel over his tomb. In time he came to be revered as a saint. His heart was said to be buried at Windsor Castle where King Edward III founded the Knights of The Garter in his honour.

And so, the noble Knight became the Patron Saint of England. His colours, a red cross upon a white background are still the flag of the realm and are part of the Union Jack.

A FAIRY'S SONG

Over hill, over dale,
   Through bush, through brier,
Over park, over pale,
   Through flood, through fire:
I do wander everywhere,
   Swifter than the moon's sphere;
And I serve the fairy queen,
   To dew her orbs upon the green:
The cowslips tall her pensioners be;
   In their gold coats spots you see;
Those be rubies, fairy favours,
   In those freckles live their savours,
I must go seek some dewdrops here,
   And hang a pearl in every cowslip's ear.

William Shakespeare

FAIRIES

"Fairies small, two feet tall, with caps of red upon their heads" was an old description for the smaller weavers of charms and spells. However, fairies came in all shapes and sizes, from finger-small to human-tall, and were capable of such rapid movement people mistook them for a moth, or a flash of light, a falling star, or a drift of dandelion seeds. Because fairies were mostly about at night and, during the day, were capable of appearing as cats, mice or other creatures — even humans — they avoided discovery by inquisitive and prying people.

You will know, I'm sure, that there were good fairies and wicked ones, and those that weren't too bad. Some were beautiful, some ugly, some kind and generous, some vicious and teasingly cruel, especially when annoyed.

As for flying, some had wings and some didn't, but they could ride on grass stalks, or a floating thistle-down puff blown by the wind.

Clever, fantastic little beings whose whereabouts are still only known to very special people! So should you ever meet a Pisky or Pillywiggins, a Redcap or a Fay, a Pixy, a Brownie, a Leprechaun or Robin Goodfellow, Puck or Ariel, Sleigh-beggey or Tylwyth Teg, then to be sure, you'll know a nimble-footed sprite. And there are others with their own special names.

TYLWYTH TEG

Once, in the time when fairies danced undisturbed, the Tylwyth Teg flittered across the moor in the white moonlight. They whooped and laughed. Over the heather tops! Over the boulders! Skipping, dancing, leaping, they whisked round in a ring until their twinkle-toed feet wore away the grass.

Then, when their loudest shrieks, hardly noisier than a pee-wit's call, mind you, shrilled with excitement, a drunken farmer stumbled into their midst. "Well, I'll be blessed! If it isn't the Little Ones!" he chuckled. "There's s-sairies all about old S-sam!" he told them and crashed to the ground.

The Tylwyth Teg were outraged. The clumsy huge oaf! The bumble-footed giant! The black-haired monster! He slept as if dead. His pig-snores drowned the lilt of their pipes. His sour breath sickened them with the stink of hops and tobacco and fried onions! *Pppt!* The stupid human spoilt their joy!

Fairy-wise they dealt with Sam.

Some fetched gossamer ropes. They flitted and crawled about him, stretching, pulling, knotting and tying until he was bound from head to toe. Now some dragged and some pushed until Sam was hauled off the dancing-green to a low-hung bush. They shoved him under it, hidden from their view. Fallen leaves cushioned his head. A blanket of thistle-down warmed his body and kept off the dew, but it didn't smother his offending snores.

They rasped on, spoiling the music until the drummers took up the long even rhythm of Sam's drones, then the pipes joined in to liven the tempo and tambourines tinkled a jingling accompaniment. The Tylwyth Teg waltzed and spun until day-break, relishing with serendipity the improvised sounds.

Sam's family worried and fretted when their Da didn't come home. All night long a lamp shone in a window facing the moors, and many times Ma stood in the doorway, looking for Sam trundling down the moon-lit road, or across the heather.

Morning came. The cows were milked. The eggs gathered. Breakfast was eaten and still there was no sign of Sam. Ma sent the boys to search for him, and they ran back as far as the town without finding their Da.

He slept on, under the bush, near the fairy-ring. He slept on until the return of the Tylwyth Teg. Over the moor! Over the heather tops! Over the boulders they leapt and skipped and sang. Then, they found him. Oh, the miching, topsy-turvy, flannel-nosed, old bagpipe should have long since gone home to Ma!

They unrolled the thistle-down blanket. They untied the gossamer ropes. They tickled his chin with a bird's feather, tweaked his nose and prodded and pinched but Sam still slept.

A troop of them took his cap to the spring and filled it with water, icy-cold and dew-fresh, which they sprinkled over his

face. Sam shuddered. He crawled from the shelter. They pushed him to his feet and he wimbled and wambled about the moors, in every direction but home. And they flitted like moths, blowing in his eyes, whispering in his ears, tugging at his hair, doing their best to send him on the right path.

The Tylwyth Teg left Sam at dawn and in the early greyness of damp mist Sam saw his house and toddled home, remembering nothing and never recalling his chance meeting with the Tylwyth Teg who kept on dancing on their green, no more than a shout away from Sam's own door.

135

COULD IT HAVE BEEN A SHADOW?

What ran under the rosebush?
What ran under the stone?
Could it have been a shadow?
Running away alone?
Maybe a fairy's shadow
Slipping away at dawn,
To guard a gleaming pot of gold
For a busy leprechaun.

Monica Shannon

LEPRECHAUN GOLD

Once, in the old times, Tom FitzPatrick went a-walking and a-seeing. Instead he heard a-tapping which was very like a tinkle, yes, a tinkle.

"Save us!" whispered Tom, keeping himself very still. "What in the world is that now? Not a grasshopper, I'll be bound."

Softly, softly he searched and poked amongst the grass blades and weeds, then crawled through the hedge, snagging his breeches. *Tap!* Tap! *Tap*pity! It was the tiniest of wee sounds to follow and only Tom's sharp ears told his eyes where to look. And there, sitting as large as life, on a three-legged stool, hunched a wee bit of a chap, dressed from top to toe in a lovely green colour, and wearing an apron and a top hat, as well. *Tap!* Tap! *Tap*pity! What was he doing but hammering at a fairy shoe, mending a hole worn in its sole with a wee scrap of fine leather.

"It's a Leprechaun, it is!" breathed Tom FitzPatrick. "And dangerous it is for an Irishman not to believe in one!"

He dared not take his eyes off the fairy-man and watched the Leprechaun bend to take up a clay jug as brown as a tree-root, and a goblet shining all over like gold. Into the goblet he poured something light and brown and very wet. Tom's nose wrinkled, appreciating the whiff of it. Up went the goblet under the long ugly nose and the Leprechaun drank. *Slllrp!* "Haaaaa!" He happily wiped his beard. "Haaaaa!" He rubbed the goblet on his apron.

"Ahhhh!" thought Tom, remembering that only Leprechauns knew how to find the pot of gold at the rainbow's end. "Good-day to you, Master!" he called as bold as a brass button.

"Good-day to you, Tom!" answered the Leprechaun without lifting his head from his work. "How are you, may I ask?"

"I'd be better for a sip of what you have in that jug," grinned Tom.

"Help yourself to a droppie."

"Here's health!" toasted Tom and he drained the jug. It was a lovely mouthful, and it sent a warmth rushing through Tom until he tingled down to his toes and felt like a song and a jig. "That's a fine lively brew!" he praised. "The best I've tasted. Where did you get it, Liddle 'un?"

"I made it. I made it from heather tops."

"Never you did! I'd like another thimble-ful if it's all the same to you."

"It doesn't suit me to give you another drop, you big greedy buffoon! You drained the jug dry. Now be off! Your cow's gone from the barn, and she's ambling down the road, she is."

"Fibs! I won't be tricked with a lie!" smirked Tom, and he grabbed the Leprechaun in both hands. He yelled, oh, he yelled. He squirmed, too, and kicked, then walloped Tom with his hammer. It wasn't any harder than a love-smack but Tom danced about with the shock of it, trampling the goblet, breaking the brown jug to shards and sending the little stool flying. He didn't let go of his Leprechaun prize but held him so tight the poor wee thing could hardly shriek.

"Now, my liddle-run-under-the-hedge, I'll hold you fast until you tell where the buried treasure be lying," said Tom leering into the little old face.

"I know of no treasure," shouted the Leprechaun.

"Any more fibs and I'll bash your head," threatened Tom and he shook the poor mite until its head shook like a rag dolly's, and it groaned for mercy.

138

"I'll show you the field of gold," the Leprechaun promised.

"Then, we'll be going," said Tom FitzPatrick, grinning his pleasure, and tying the belt from his breeches round the Leprechaun's middle before he put him on the ground.

Then they were off. And a merry dance it was. Over the fields, under the hedges, by the bog, through the bracken patch — with Tom clutching one end of the belt in one hand and his breeches in the other. At last they were in the forty-acre potato field. A great field of taties! Uncounted plants of spuds!

The Leprechaun hopped straight to a certain plant somewhere near the middle of the field. "Under that one!" he mumbled. "Dig there!"

"Then it's home for me spade!" chortled Tom. And what does he then do? Whipped off his raggedy, torn, red garter of ancient age and while his sock fell down he tied the garter to the tatie plant with a twist and a loop. "Will you swear that you'll never be touchin' me garter?" he asked.

"I swear," vowed the Leprechaun. "Will you be letting me go then?"

"Sure, you can go." Tom undid his belt. "Be on your way, now."

The Leprechaun went in a flash to some hidden root, or ruined castley place in Ireland, the lovely homeland which Leprechauns never, never leave.

Tom FitzPatrick capered off too, still holding his breeches — through the bracken patch, by the bog, over the hedge and across the fields to be met by his wandering cow, dreamily travelling over the grass. "He told me you were out!" puffed Tom. "And so you are."

He hauled her back to the barn, fetched his spade and was away once more. Down the road, across the fields, over the hedge, by the bog, through the bracken patch — into the forty-acre field of taties.

Eeeeeek! Tom howled like a banshee. He chucked down his spade. Stamped and kicked until he was brown with dust and it filled his nose and eyes. Poor Tom! Every potato plant wore on its greenness a ragged red garter. Every garter matched Tom's own, whichever one that was.

He gritted his teeth and he dug and he dug. He dug until evening. He dug in the moonlight. He dug the next day and the next until he dug up the field. Ahhhh! it was a sad time for Tom FitzPatrick! He never found the treasure. Never!

POTATO TRICK

Here's a potato trick which may or may not be known
to the Leprechauns.

You will need:
   a glass
   a small potato
   two forks which should be twins
Spear the potato with the forks as near as you
can to being closely opposite and at the same
angle. Put the potato and the forks over the
glass, on the very edge. Will it balance there?
It should.
Can you work out why?

LINSEY-WOOLSEY BROWNIE

He was no taller than the leg of a kitchen chair. He was brown all over, covered completely in hair, except for his wrinkled, criss-crossed face which looked as old as last autumn's apple, but then Brownie, bless his bright twinkling eyes, was more than three hundred years old.

For most of those years he had lived in the same farmhouse, quietly going about his chores when good folk were sleeping in their beds. Brownie loved to work and he asked for no thanks, except a bowl of cream and a hot-buttered cake to be left on the hearth each evening. Many a Good Wife left him his share of a family treat as well. He deserved it. Everyone knew that the luck of the house depended upon Brownie. He milked the cows, churned the butter, mowed the hay, comforted sick animals and kept everything running smoothly as long as he was left alone.

But woe betide the lass who left the kitchen as clean as a whistle! Tidiness turned Brownie into a thwarted bouncing fur-ball. He stormed about the room. Crashed the pile of clean dishes. Holed the porridge pot. Stole the cupboard keys. Kicked the cat. Scattered cinders. Broke the churn and hid the baby's rattle. Then, insulted and offended, Brownie stalked off into a hidey-hole to sulk. Wasn't it his duty to look after the kitchen? Wasn't he a valued member of the household?

Indeed, he was, he was. And one evening, a young and new and very inexperienced Lady-of-the-House couldn't sleep. She slipped to the Kitchen to make a warm drink when she heard Brownie complaining bitterly,

"Wae's me, wae's me!
The acorn's not yet
Fallen from the tree
That's to grow the wood
That's to make the cradle
That's to grow the bairn
That's to be the man
That's to lay me!"

Huddled as small as a cushion, Brownie rocked in misery before the hearth. And in the flickering fire-light naked skin showed through sparse brown hair.

"The poor wee thing! I'd best be making something to warm his old back," the Young Wife told herself and crept back to bed.

The good woman had recently spun a web of linsey-woolsey. Oh, it was soft and feather-fine and just the thing! Next morning she snipped enough from the end of her cloth to cut breeches and a coat with a hood. She stitched it all to Brownie-sized clothes and laid them on the hearth that same evening.

He found her gift when he came for his cream. Slowly he dressed and as he fastened the buttons on the coat Brownie burst into sobs,

"Poor Brownie! Poor Brownie!
With new trews, coat and hood.
Poor Brownie! Poor Brownie!
He'll nae work as he should."

Wailing sorrowfully he left the house, taking the good luck of the place with him. The mice broke into the flour bag. The cow ailed. The hens went off the lay. Milk soured. Cakes burned. "No man could lay our Brownie," grieved the Farmer. "It took a slip of a lass with a gift of clothes to send him flitting. Girlie! Girlie, a Brownie should *never* be paid!" And they tried to lure him back with choice morsels which dried on the hearth. Brownie was gone, gone for good.

Then, years later, Farmer was milking when Brownie, tattered and raggy, poked his head into the dairy asking, "Will you kindly give me the loan of your horse and cart, Sir?"

"The horse is nothing but a skinny old nag and the cart not much of a cart. Things have been poorly," said Farmer.

"Then I'll take them for a wee while. The place where I am doesn't suit me," Brownie whined. "It's the noise of the ding-dongs ting-tanging in the village church. My littlings can't sleep and their mither complains."

"You're welcome. You worked long enough here to deserve the use of my gear. It's only a loan. We can't afford to give."

Brownie flitted once more, and where he went no one knew, but it must have been away from the sound of the village ding-dongs.

He returned the horse, sleek and fat and spry enough for another ten years. He returned the cart, repaired and painted, strong enough for another ten years.

After that, the affairs of the farm were better. Everything thrived, and the seasons were good again. Everyone grew happy and fat.

THE LITTLE OLD MAN OF THE BARN

When the peat will turn grey and shadows fall deep
And weary Old Callum is snoring asleep . . .
The Little Old Man of the Barn
Will thresh with no light in the mouth of the night,
The Little Old Man of the Barn.

BUG-A-BOO BOGGART

People who know such things say that a Boggart is a Brownie who has gone bad. And one such Boggart was a real Bug-a-boo to a kindly Farmer and his family.

For some reason Bug-a-boo took a dislike to the children. He snatched bread and butter from their little hands and threw it down in the dirt, turned their soup bowls upside down, threw their spoons out of the window, tore holes in their clothes, tweaked at shirts and skirts, tugged plaits, tied hair in knots and slyly pinched and poked. No one saw him do any of these things, so blamed the closest sister or brother for the teasings. There was no peace in the house. No peace!

Sometimes, the children thought they saw the Boggart. He wore a ragged green coat and a green cap, said the smallest child. She had seen him dancing to a cricket's chirrup. Yes, it was Bug-a-boo and not a birdie fluttering through a bush.

146

And once, the biggest boy thought he saw a scowling-ugly, floor-mop of a face glaring at him through the big crack in the little door under the stairs. It had pointed ears and a turned-down nose, and crossed eyes and red hair which stood around its head every-which-way. Everyone knew that Bug-a-boo looked like that. "Leave us alone!" he told the face and poked a shoe-horn through the crack.

Back flew the shoe-horn. It struck the lad's shoulder. Ooooh! It hurt and he ran yelping to his mother.

Sometimes, when Bug-a-boo felt generous he helped with the farm work. More often he teased the cattle worse than flies, tangled the harness, spilled the grain and threw dung in the milk. Half the day was spent undoing the Boggart's mischief.

"We'll have to quit this place," moaned the Farmer's Wife. "There is no peace from the Boggart."

"I'm not quitting. I'll make a bargain with that little devil, then we'll have peace," declared the Farmer.

And next morning he shouted through the barn door, "You behave yourself, Bug-a-boo, and you can have half the crop in the big field."

"Aye! It's a bargain if you do all the work," Bug-a-boo yelled back.

"Which half will you have then? Tops or bottoms?"

"Bottoms!"

"Then bottoms you'll have. Done!"

Bug-a-boo did behave himself. He kept his word. So did the Farmer. He planted wheat and when harvest time came he took the grain and left the roots for Bug-a-boo, and even a Boggart can't use a mesh of roots.

"Plant another crop," he screeched, "and this time I'll have tops."

Farmer planted turnips and at harvest time he took the roots and left a pile of green leafy tops for Bug-a-boo. His language was not fit to be heard by any ears. "This time I'll not have tops and I'll not have bottoms!" he told the Farmer. "You will plant corn. Corn, do you hear? And the whole harvest goes to the winner of a mowing match!"

Oh, dear, dear, dear! No man alive can beat a Boggart at mowing, and sure of victory, Bug-a-boo buzzed about the field supervising it into perfect halves and pausing only to frighten the children with a couple of screeches, or well-placed pinches.

Next morning, bright and early, Boggart and Farmer took their positions. One-two-three! The match began. Up and down his patch the Farmer worked steadily, his mower moving sweetly and evenly.

Bug-a-boo made a flying start, then was stopped time and again by a hundred snags. Things kept catching at the mower, blunting the blades until they couldn't cut. He raged and kicked about, then hollered, "When do we wiffle-waffle, Farmer?"

"At noon."

"Noon! I'll never be finished. The field's yours!" And Bug-a-boo retired, defeated, and in a hurry to reach his hiding hole.

Had he stayed he would have seen the Farmer pulling thin iron rods from Bug-a-boo's side of the field — the snags, his bothersome snags.

Later, Bug-a-boo sidled sheepishly into the kitchen to find a welcoming bowl of cream. And afterwards there was peace in the house. Both Boggart and children treated each other with kindness and respect, as friends usually do.

148

THE CRITTER GOT AWAY

Gaily

"Who's been mess - ing up the oats?" Yelled a Farm - er,

cuss - ing oaths. Saw a Gob - lin, tried to lob him!

But the crit - ter got a - way.

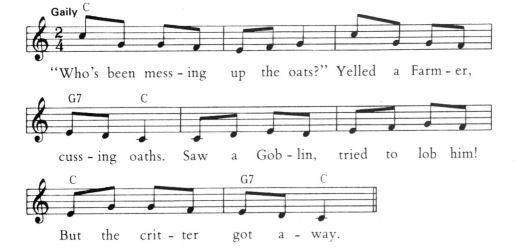

"Who's been pulling up the corn?"
Yelled a Farmer one fine morn
Saw a Boggart, almost got it!
But the critter got away.

Yelled the Farmer, "What's the use?
Critters ruin what I produce.
Goblin, Boggart, I have had it!"
And the Farmer went away.

THE GOBLIN

A goblin lives in *our* house, in *our* house, in *our* house,
A goblin lives in our house all the year round.
He bumps
And he jumps
And he thumps
And he stumps.
He knocks
And he rocks
And he rattles at the locks.
A goblin lives in our house, in our house, in our house,
A goblin lives in our house all the year round.

Rose Fyleman

DISAPPEARING BOGGART

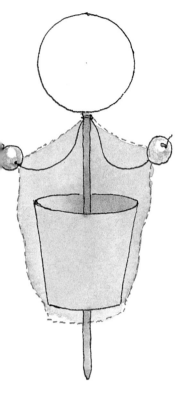

To make a Boggart you will need:
  a yoghurt carton or a small drink can
  a piece of dowelling about 35cm long and
    pencil-thin
  some string
  scraps of red material
  two macrame beads, and some glue,
  cotton wool, or something for hair,
  and perhaps an adult helper.
  a ping-pong ball

Ask someone to help you to push the dowel through the bottom of the carton. Push the top of the dowel into the ball. This is the head.

Just below the head, tie the string so that the ends are of equal length. These are arms. Knot the macrame beads to the ends of the string arms.

To make the Boggart's clothes, cut the material twice as long as the carton and a little more than the measurement around its widest part. Glue or gather one narrow end of the cloth to the dowel, just below the head.

Glue or gather the arms into place. Be sure that the bead-hands are on the outside.

Glue the bottom of the gown to the *bottom* of the carton. You can neaten the edge by finishing it off with some braid.

Give the Boggart some hair. Draw on a face. Leave him to dry.

Now pull the dowel stick down as far as it will go. The Boggart disappears inside. Push up the stick and back he pops.

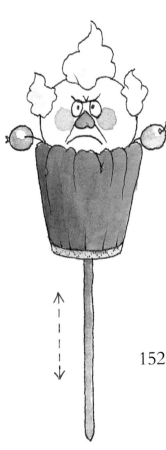

152

APPLE-TREE MAN

Once, in the topsy-turvy world, a younger son inherited the
family fortune when his father up and died. The farm was his,
and the animals, the house and all the odds and ends.

First thing he did, the young scoundrel, was to turn out his
brother, John. Put him right out of the house. Now that set
the village tongues wagging and prattling. So, to prove that he
wasn't a flint-hearted, mean misery, he made a big to-do
about giving John one horse, one ox and the use of the
ramshackle old hut at the end of the orchard. Rent was to be
paid, on the knocker, every Christmas.

John was a hard-worker, as everyone knew, and he was no
complainer which was perhaps a pity. The horse was a
broken-down old nag, unfit for work. The ox was even older,
with tottery legs and no strength left; the hut was older than
both the animals put together. It had been tumbling down for
years. Even more ancient still were three apple trees which
grew near the hut. Gnarled and bowed by the years, they
hadn't borne fruit for seasons.

153

Well, John hied up to the orchard with the animals and then he took his scythe to cut grass in the lane. It was sweet and juicy, exactly to the ox's liking. Next, sweet herbs were found for the horse.

After their bellies were filled and rested John brushed and combed away mud and tangles, which made the beasts feel so comfortable they perked up no end. Soon, they roamed the orchard completely at peace with the world. And they kept a friendly eye on their master's doings too, often browsing close to him while he pruned the apple trees.

John cut out dead wood and shortened over-long branches. The trees were soon a trim shape and after John weeded about their roots and gave them a good feed of manure they began to send out new shoots. They thrived just like the animals.

By autumn John had turned his hand to repairing the hut, banging and hammering and splashing paint about. By Christmas the hut was a little house but John had had no time to earn the money to pay his rent. His brother was bound to want it. Right on the knocker and no excuses! So payment day and Christmas Eve arrived together. So did the young brother, bashing on the door and yelling. "I've come for the rent. You haven't got it, have you?"

"No," said John.

"I knew it, and I'll forget part of it on one condition."

"What's that?"

"It's Christmas Eve, and everyone knows it is the night when beasts are given the gift of speech."

"So it is said," agreed John. "They shared their stable with the Holy Family on the first Christmas and were so honoured."

"That is a fact. It is also known that there is a buried treasure hereabouts. Finders are keepers, so I'm all set to ask your old horse where it lies. If he refuses, then I'll turn the lot of you out."

"But it will be Christmas Day."

"I know it," shrugged the brother. "Listen now! It'll be worth your while if the horse speaks the secret. I'll take six pennies off the rent."

Oh, yes, he was a generous man who would make a fortune before he died. Pleased with his bargain, he left.

John considered what had been said, and he was sure that this would be the last night he'd spend in the orchard. Still, he busied himself with the animals, fetching them extra rations, which was an old Christmas custom in those parts. The horse and ox got both carrots and hay, and a sprig of holly pinned over the stable door, as well. John had another piece over his doorway for good luck, and very bright it looked there when he went into the little place, to tip up the cider barrel, draining its dregs into a mug. It wasn't to drink. Goodness, no! He took the mug straight to the orchard. And although it would have tasted well on his tongue and warmed up his insides, he poured it about the roots of the three apple trees, just as had been done in the old days, like a Christmas blessing or a thank you for good harvests.

The cider soaked into the soil and, as the damp patch widened, the oldest tree seemed to stir, then fidget. The bare branches crackled restlessly, bent towards John and faint whisperings, like rustling leaves, fell upon his ears. "Look under this great root of mine, John. Look now!"

The earth moved at John's feet, parting with a little falling of dead leaves and soil to reveal a knobbled root which looped upwards. Under the loop lay a chest.

"Pull it out!" whispered the voice and John looked up to a kindly face squinting down at him from the fretwork of branches — a kindly face of ancient yellow, a shrunken apple-face, round and small.

"You're the Apple-tree Man!" said John.

"That be so. You awakened me with the cider gift and you have given new life to three old trees. Help yourself to that chest now. We kept it for the likes of you, kept it hidden for long years."

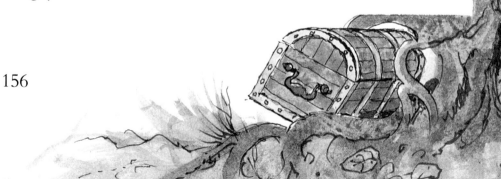

John took up the chest, re-covered the root with soil, which he tamped down firmly with his boot, then, advised by the Apple-tree Man, took the chest to his house.

Close on midnight his Brother came running through the orchard, pushing by the Apple-tree Man to burst into the stable. To his astonishment the ox was talking to the horse, in a soft lowing, well-mannered fashion. "John's brother is a fool, you could say. You would remember him, old friend?"

"I remember him, and if you declare he is a fool then I agree," answered the horse. "What has he done now?"

"No more than he planned," went on the ox. "He expects you to reveal where the treasure is buried."

"I could, but it would do him no good. He could dig for a year and still not find it," whinnied the horse.

"Then there is treasure in the orchard?" asked the ox.

"In the sweet grass and the apple crops there is treasure enough for some, but never the greedy." Now the horse's neigh sounded like laughter. He stamped a foot and flung back his head. "*Someone has already taken the treasure!*"

The younger brother had not missed a word. And what did the miserable creature do but turn the animals out into the frosty night. Then, he evicted his brother from the house.

John found a warm inn to stay with shelter for the horse and the ox. In the chest filled with coins and other valuables, there was more than enough to set himself up very nicely on a nearby farm, and when times were bad for his young brother, he bought from him the orchard and the three ancient apple trees. So that was that!

CHARM TO GROW MORE APPLES

Here stands a good apple tree!
Stand fast at root,
Bear well at top,
Every little twig
Bear an apple big;
Every little bough
Bear an apple now;
Hats full! Caps full!
Full quarter sacks full!
And my breeches pockets full!
Hey-hey! Hello!

APPLE-EATERS-SAVE-THOSE-SEEDS!

Apple-eaters, save the seeds.
Ask others to save theirs. Wash them.
Dry them. Thread them into a long glossy
necklace. It makes a good present for someone
you like. Or make a bracelet — that takes less
seeds, and you need *lots* for both, but then,
apples are good to eat.

FINIS

Night is come,
Owls are out,
Beetles hum
Run about:

Children snore
Safe in bed,
Nothing more
Need be said.

Sir Henry Newbolt

Goodnight!
Sleep tight!

INDEX